A NICKEL FOR THE BOATMAN

A NICKEL FOR THE BOATMAN

A Novel

Carol Luter Milot

authorHOUSE®

AuthorHouse™
1663 Liberty Drive
Bloomington, IN 47403
www.authorhouse.com
Phone: 1-800-839-8640

First published by AuthorHouse   11/04/2011

ISBN: 978-1-4670-3836-2 (sc)
ISBN: 978-1-4670-3837-9 (hc)
ISBN: 978-1-4670-3838-6 (ebk)

Library of Congress Control Number: 2011916868

Printed in the United States of America

Author's note: Most of the characters and incidents in this novel are products of the author's imagination. The words and actions of any historical figures as depicted in this story are purely fictitious, with the exception of James Alderman's letter of regret, which was reproduced exactly as originally published in The Miami Herald. Any historical events mentioned herein have been well researched by the author and have been depicted as accurately as possible.

For my father B. F. Parker, whose intelligence, wit, and love of beauty have inspired me throughout my life.

ACKNOWLEDGMENTS

The idea for this book came from a lifetime of conversations with my father, B.F. Parker, whose stories of Miami in the early days thrilled and inspired me. While this novel is a work of fiction, many of the descriptions of people, places and events were drawn directly from his experiences and recollections.

The book could never have been completed without the encouragement I received from friends and family throughout the entire process from inception to completion. Special thanks go to: my husband Andy for listening, listening and listening again; my friend Carolyn Reedy for her help proofreading and spotting inconsistencies; to Dee and Len Sonier for their sensitive and encouraging critical feedback; especially to my editor Nan Spires, whose insight helped pull together a loosely composed manuscript into a tighter, more readable novel, and to her husband Rick Keaton, who knows more about life and death than anyone should and helped us both understand the feelings in that critical moment when death is upon you. Finally, to my former students who acted as a test audience for a chapter or two: THANK YOU. HERE IT IS. FINALLY.

It wouldn't change anything, but just the same I wish we had been warned . . . sooner or later innocence dies.

Anonymous

PROLOGUE

Heat waves shimmer above the shallow water of the Everglades transforming the endless expanse of saw grass into an insubstantial landscape, an elusive mirage. Even the solemn faces of the two priests standing just in front of him seem to waver before his eyes like reflections on the surface of a puddle.

"The wages of sin is death. The African said it," one priest pronounces solemnly over the boy's bowed head. The other ties his hands behind his back and deftly wraps the rope several times around his chest pulling it taut like a boatswain securing a dock line. The boy swallows hard and tries not to cry.

The priest goes on, "There is a price to enter the underworld, my son." As if administering communion, he raises a nickel toward the frightened boy's face and places it on his tongue.

The rough coils of rope squeeze his chest, cutting off his air until his lungs burn with each push of labored breath. A sound gutters up from his throat. It began as an airless, hoarse whimper between gasps but emerges as a startling scream.

He awoke with a violent start to the sound of his own voice. Jerking upright, the old man thrashed to free his body from a tangle of damp bedclothes. As he groped about for his glasses on the nightstand, his shaking hand sent a cluster of pill bottles clattering onto the floor.

Now through his glasses, the dim, indistinct outlines of objects became clearer. As his eyes adjusted to the darkness, the spiny creature crouching in the shadows slowly came into focus and morphed into a fat jar of sharpened pencils resting on the corner worktable. Next to it, the threatening cobra on the wall dissolved into the shadow of the gooseneck lamp sitting on his bureau beneath a cluster of framed awards reading *The Knights of Columbus*. Above those, an ornately engraved St. Vincent DePaul Society's "Top Fundraiser" plaque inscribed with his name, Edward Boyd, came into focus and brought him completely into the present.

As he recognized the familiar, mundane objects he began to breathe more easily. He willed his pulse to slow to a more normal rate remembering the doctor's admonition, underscored by words like heart attack and stroke, warning him to avoid strenuous physical activity and stress.

He knew that at eighty-nine he was unlikely to engage in strenuous physical activity, not when a simple act like putting on shoes was tantamount to a labor of Hercules. And he could count on his stiff joints to remind him to slow down on the rare occasion when he felt frisky yet forgetful. No, it wasn't physical exertion that would eventually get him. It was the other thing, one he couldn't control, that caused him to hyperventilate and become light-headed even when awake.

He slowly lifted each leg over the side of the bed. Finally upright, he ran gnarled, crooked fingers through thin wisps of white hair and knotted his hands into fists to scrub his rheumy eyes. He listened to the familiar rasp of the sweaty stubble on his cheeks and chin under the movement of his palm. Readjusting his glasses, he squinted at the alarm clock. TIME: 3:18 A.M. He exhaled and lay back poking the damp pillow under his neck.

2

The same version of the dream had wrenched him from sleep for the third time in as many nights. He turned over pulling the covers tightly around his shoulders and lay listening. The hollow silence that always followed the dreams had once been oppressive, but this time it reminded him that he wasn't his home's lone occupant anymore. He hoped he hadn't awakened Diana.

He had not always lived alone, but it had been many, many years since he'd shared this house with anyone. There had been a time, what was it now, fifty, sixty years ago, when he'd thought he might have a wife, family, and a normal life. For a short while it had seemed he could.

The brief respite had lasted for only a year after his marriage before the dreams began again. And with their return, an underlying resentment germinated, inevitably choking off any possibility of success the relationship might have had. Back then, he rationalized it was the nightmares that had driven the wedge between them. But he now conceded it was the wall he alone had built around himself that turned the rift into a gulf too wide to bridge.

In their early years together when his wife had been concerned and reached out to him on nights like this, he had turned his back on her. None of her efforts or repeated coaxing had been enough to break down the wall of silence. That his reticence had only to do with him and nothing to do with her was something he couldn't explain. He simply didn't know how.

Even when he could clearly see the hurt and confusion in her eyes, he had ignored it and buried his head in the sand avoiding confrontation by pretending not to notice. Finally, in the seventh year of their marriage, when she walked out with five-year-old Diana and two-year-old Sam, he was admittedly hurt but hardly surprised. He was almost a little relieved.

He had kept in touch with the children over the years, sending cards and gifts for holidays, birthdays and graduations. He'd been there at the church for their mother's funeral, sitting in a pew near the back out of respect for her family's wishes. But he never dreamed then that the day would come when he'd find himself dependent upon one of his children. Funny, he thought, how at his age life had still held back a few surprises.

As his heart rate returned to normal and the adrenaline subsided, he willed himself to relax, to let the tension drain from his arms and legs. But on this night, the nightmare had released a flood of memories that seeped back in, filling every corner of his mind. After a few minutes of tossing and turning, he abandoned any further futile attempts to fall into sleep.

He sat back up, rose stiffly to his feet, and looked around. Where was his cane? He couldn't remember where he had left it. These days, simple tasks like walking were becoming increasingly uncertain. If he didn't want to wake his daughter, he'd have to be careful not to stumble over something on his way to the kitchen. He shut his door gently and padded softly down the hall, keeping one hand on the wall to steady him.

Only a couple of months ago, he'd taken a serious fall that should have put him in a nursing home. Had it not been for Diana's insistence on moving in to care for him, he would be there now. Refusing to listen to his protests, she had packed up and moved into his house in Little Havana. After all, she argued, who needed her now more than he did? She had been divorced and living on her own for fifteen years, and her children had their own lives.

In spite of his stubborn insistence that he needed no help and that when he left his home it would be toes up on a gurney, the fall had scared him more than he liked to admit. After two months of her unshakable persistence, they had grudgingly reached a truce, and now, in spite of his many misgivings, here they were—a pair of unlikely roommates.

Surprisingly, it had proved to be an arrangement he found tolerable. At times, he'd even begun to enjoy the company although he'd never admit it. A further bonus he hadn't anticipated was Diana's fluency in Spanish.

When he had moved into this house in 1952, the area had been all Anglo. But by 1970, so many Cuban refugees had settled in this sprawling neighborhood west of downtown Miami stretching west from the Miami River for several miles that it had been dubbed Little Havana. In 2000, the last non-Cuban neighbor had moved away from this old enclave of modest bungalows leaving him the only holdout.

Since he had never attempted to learn a single word of Spanish, he barely communicated with his neighbors other than the occasional nod when it couldn't be avoided. He'd secretly begun to worry that if his heart conked out, he wouldn't be able to call to anyone living nearby for help. Within days of her arrival, though, Diana had made friends with several Spanish-speaking neighbors, so he could now put that fear to rest.

A floorboard creaked. He turned to see her shuffle into the kitchen pulling her chenille robe around her shoulders.

"Can't sleep, Dad?" she asked, yawning. "Me either," she went on, setting the coffee pot to brew. She stood at the counter with her back to him.

"I thought I heard someone shout," she said matter-of-factly.

"Oh, well, you know the dreams of an old man can sometimes make him think he's young again," he smiled sheepishly.

She turned, raised an eyebrow and shot him a look of clear disbelief.

"No, not that," he confessed. "I think I was dreaming of fishing."

Purposely diverting her attention, he took off his glasses, plucked a napkin from the center of the table and deliberately wiped the lenses.

"Where is your cane?" she asked looking around the kitchen. "You know it isn't safe to walk without it, especially when you're sneaking around the house in the dark."

"I couldn't find it, AND I wasn't sneaking."

She carried two mugs of coffee and two spoons to the table, slid the sugar bowl between them, and sat across from him.

"Seriously," she prodded, "You're sure you're okay? Sometimes I hear noises in the night and I'm afraid you're sick and calling me. I swear, Dad, sometimes I worry that you'll up and die on me before we've even gotten to know each other."

He stared into his coffee mug, more than a little stung by her words. He knew well he had clearly not been much of a parent and admittedly lacked many other virtues as well. He had tried all his life, though, to make up for his failings by being a good Catholic. He had gone to church and to confession regularly. He had given his time to the poor even if he hadn't given much of it to his own children.

What did he owe this daughter of his who was nearly a stranger to him? Why did she uproot her life and come here to take care of him, an old man she'd hardly known? There were things about him she could never understand. Things he'd kept bottled up for nearly a lifetime. Secrets, yes there *were* secrets he had shared with no one, not even in the darkness of the confessional.

He looked up at her intently. Their hands cradling the hot mugs shared the same long, blunt fingers. Diana's knuckles were already showing signs of the arthritis that had gnarled his hands, although the backs of hers were not yet marred by liver spots and enlarged blue veins, a clear sign of his advanced years.

"Well, what do you want to know?" He said it softly, almost willingly.

"So many things," Diana began gently, as if she were about to peel a bandage from a painful wound and needed to proceed with extreme care. She looked at him earnestly and leaned forward, her elbows on the table, her chin resting on her clasped hands. "Even though I was so little when you and Mama divorced," she went on, "I felt hurt, you know? Sam and I didn't understand, and Mama would never talk about it. When we would ask her about you, she'd just say, 'Your father was a closed book,' as if that explained everything."

"I guess she resented the fact," he mused, staring into his cup, "that for all her trying, she was never able to pry my cover open and didn't understand why. But then, there was a lot about me she didn't understand." When he didn't speak again for a long moment, Diana had to stifle an impulse to prod him with another question.

"I think what attracted me to her," he finally went on, "was that she was everything I wasn't. She grew up in a big, close-knit family. They all seemed to know how to laugh and enjoy life. I imagined by marrying her I could catch that spark, you know? Ironic, really." He paused, twisting his napkin around two fingers. "What drew me to her is what pushed her away from me." He was silent again for a time.

"My parents weren't anything like that," he finally continued softly, an oblique glance pulling him into another time and place. "There was always this distance between them. I don't think I ever saw them openly affectionate. They didn't even talk much to each other, and less often to me."

Then, as if shaking himself free of his reverie, "You may not have understood it back then," he said with a smile, "but you were lucky your mother and I divorced. Even though she never remarried, Mama had her big family around her and so did you and Sam." His gaze traveled over her face, settling finally on her eyes. "You're very like her. Did you know that?"

Diana shook her head responding to his question. "No, not really. Sometimes people said I looked like her, but not that I *was* like her. I always suspected she thought I was more like you."

"It was as if . . ." she began. Now it was his turn to wait.

"I always had the feeling that Mama never felt accepted by Grandmother and Grandfather Boyd. She never said it, but I think she thought your family considered hers somehow beneath them. Were your parents very rich?"

His expression clouded over again.

"Well, if wishes were fishes, they'd have had a boatload," he said.

He leaned back and allowed his thoughts to slide down the archeological strata into his past. His mind shoveled aside regret and gently brushed the undisturbed years from the oldest timbers of his memory.

Diana watched as this sifting sent a sundial of shadows across his face. She said nothing allowing the silence to stretch on. Just as she had begun to fear she had pushed him too far too fast, he cleared his throat and his eyes again met hers.

When he began again, his voice took on an unfamiliar tone that signaled sincerity. In his dimly lit kitchen, in the wee dark hours just before dawn, seemed as good a place and time as any to make an honest beginning.

PART ONE

Eddie

ONE

The Great War had just ended when Edward Boyd, Sr. moved his new bride Anne to Miami from Tennessee promising that it would be a great place to raise a family. But like most new transplants who had succumbed to the Magic City's seductive smile, the Boyds had arrived to discover that life there was going to be much less carefree and far more ambiguous than they had expected.

The local residents in those days were a hodge-podge bunch that ran the whole gamut of society: hardy pioneers who had braved the Seminoles and hacked down palm thickets to build a town; poor black and Bahamian laborers who worked for them; the rich and famous who came seasonally to enjoy the tropical winters; the corrupt, who would flock to any venue where they could use their wits or their muscle to get something for nothing. And of course the many hopeful lower and middle class working people like the Boyds.

Like so many others upon their arrival, they, too, were approached by the real estate hucksters who were busy selling lots, many under water, to buyers mostly from the North eager to own a piece of the American Dream. Only old-timers remember now that during the height of the real estate boom, most properties changed hands on paper at least three or four times. They were sold on "a binder", a contract that required 10% down with the balance due in ninety days. Sometimes, in a week or two, the price had gone up enough for a tidy profit, and the binder would be resold to a second buyer who paid whatever the never ending stream of the unsuspecting would bear. Worse, the balance was due in an even shorter time. This frantic game of real estate hop-scotch went on until the decade ended with the crash of the stock market.

Anne and Edward Boyd had arrived in Miami without the required 10%, having spent their small nest egg on two train tickets from Nashville and the cost of moving their few modest possessions to their soon-to-be new home. By default, they had become renters.

Once settled, Anne became an intent and determined social climber. Having been born into an old, if not prominent, Nashville family, she came by it honestly. As soon as she realized she'd entered into a hasty and ill-conceived marriage, she set out to regain something of her former social position.

Anne's first glimpse of her future husband had come at a society wedding in Nashville where he was shooting the final formal portrait of her friends the bride and groom. Anne had developed a bohemian fascination with artists—a momentary lapse of judgment her father hoped—and Edward offered her a glimpse into that glamorous world she dreamed of. The handsome photographer had quickly swept her off her feet.

At the age of twenty-five, Edward Boyd had already established himself as a well-paid and sought after portrait photographer. He may have lacked money, old Southern ties and the family status of the men in Anne's circle, but his reputation opened the doors to their world. If he'd thought to secure a permanent place in it through Anne, he was mistaken. Unimpressed with the arts or Edward's reputation, the old man quickly disowned his daughter as soon as he learned that she and Edward had eloped.

After marrying and moving to Miami, Anne devoted most of her time and effort to establishing herself as a member of polite, if not upper crust, society. When she wasn't hosting teas or bridge parties, she stayed busy keeping current on the latest fashions, shopping, and spending too much of Edward's wages on an extensive wardrobe of dresses with matching hats, gloves, and shoes.

If it was the glamour of his work that had drawn Anne to Edward, photography held a very different appeal for him. He was an introvert who preferred to view life through the lens of a camera rather than participate in it directly. His darkroom was a small, detached garage behind the house that he had converted into a workspace. It provided a sanctuary where he could find solitude and escape from a growing household that now included a young son and a maid. Even when he wasn't working, little Eddie would often wander in to find him alone there, sitting quietly under the dim red light surrounded by the prints that lined his walls and worktable. On the few occasions when Eddie had asked him to explain some aspect of the mysterious processes involved in his craft, the man had shown no real enthusiasm. It was at these times that Eddie felt keenly disappointed and separate. From his child's perspective, he mistakenly assumed his father found him too intellectually or aesthetically lacking to acquire the necessary knowledge and skills of a good photographer. The truth was that given the steady stream of social gatherings hosted by his mother, sharing his interest with Eddie would have meant giving up solitary dominion over his one place of refuge, his darkroom.

While Miami had plenty of subjects to photograph, the city lacked the old money and sensibilities of the more established cultural centers in the Old South such as Charleston, Nashville, and Atlanta where Edward had been afforded a steady source of income as a portrait photographer. It wasn't long after the Boyd's move from

Nashville that Edward's commissions for portraits dwindled to just a few every other month.

Soon he was forced to take on part-time work as a freelance photographer. Rather than the prestigious commissions he had formerly commanded, he now spent most of his time snapping photographs of the prominent, rich, and notorious for *The Miami Herald's* society pages. Edward's loss of artist status crushed Anne, who felt sure her father would gloat if he knew he'd been right all along about the "boy's" potential. Anne's disappointment cast a chilly pall over her relationship with Edward, making the darkroom an even more appealing destination for him as the years passed.

Adding to these discouragements was the fact that the Boyds, whose ambitions far exceeded their prospects, seemed always to be living beyond their means. In fact, before the end of the decade, Eddie and his family would be forced to move out of four different houses (the result of delinquent rent). They moved so often that soon they were on a first name basis with the movers, who cast knowing looks behind the young couple's backs.

Despite Edward's earlier visions of having a large family, after Eddie Jr. came along there would be no other children. He was an intelligent and precocious child, yet growing up the only offspring of disillusioned, non-communicative parents and lacking the companionship of a sibling, Eddie became a loner in a city filled with lush beauty and an undercurrent of vice.

In Miami in the 1920's, an old truth reaffirmed itself: in paradise, temptation is never far away. In those days, the first northern frost sent wealthy winter residents, who the locals referred to as snow birds, scurrying south. They were eager to swim, soak up the Florida sun, go to the racetrack, and throw lavish parties for other members of their social coterie. The azure water of the Atlantic beaches and the inky blue of the Gulf Stream also attracted artists, actors, and writers like Fitzgerald and Hemingway, who came for play and sport. The Eighteenth Amendment prohibiting whiskey didn't deter them from enjoying themselves either.

The water provided easy access for rum running, a mob-controlled enterprise. With the whiskey, came the speak-easies, gambling casinos, whorehouses and other forms of vice run by Chicago mobs. Mob bosses were in a position to emulate Miami's wealthy winter elite. They moved into lavish estates and rubbed elbows with their spotlessly clean society neighbors. With the opening of the season, came the small time crooks, bookies, racetrack touts, expensive prostitutes, and back room gamblers that added another colorful layer to Miami's social milieu.

The ocean that drew this diverse population to Miami was an even more elemental part of life for the young boy growing up in such a time and place. As often as the Boyds were forced to move, they always managed to stay close to the ocean. At night through his open window, Eddie could smell the pungent odor of the changing tide wafting in with the breeze. The sea was as familiar to him as the air he breathed; its ebb and flow was as ever-present and unwavering as the steady pulsing of his heart.

*   *   *

Sitting at the kitchen table with Diana, Ed pulled in a lungful of air. All these years later he could still smell the sea. With it, he breathed in the freshness of his youth. From his earliest years, the water had an almost mesmerizing pull on him. He had immediately fallen in love with its beauty; he was much slower to appreciate its potential dangers.

His earliest days were spent pursuing idyllic pleasure and adventure. At his doorstep, lay every possible enticement to attract a curious child, and he began to explore as soon as he could walk. At the tender age of three, in spite of strict instructions from his parents not to leave the confines of the yard, he would often wander down to the water tower located just a block from his house right on the shore. On one of his frequent rambles, he climbed into an empty rowboat that had been left tied to a dock. The momentum from his clambering onboard caused the tiny vessel to drift out to the end of its mooring line. Not knowing how to swim, he sat terrified for what seemed like hours, having no idea what to do until an older boy happened by. Realizing the child's predicament, he generously pulled Eddie up onto the shore and with a cautious warning sent him walking home. As his young mind deciphered the adventure, he quickly calculated that, having disregarded his parents' instruction to stay put, he'd better keep his escapade a secret. Even then, he intuitively understood that many of his activities, mostly involving the water, would not meet with their approval.

In those days, the water of the bay was pristine and sparkling. Pods of dolphins would roll through it feeding on mullet. The hunted schools leaped into the air creating an iridescent curtain of silver as they tried to escape to shallower water. Huge manta rays were plentiful. To Eddie's amazement, occasionally one with an eight or ten-foot wingspan would silently sail out of the water only to noisily drop back onto the surface with the force of a cannon's crash. Whether this behavior was an expression of pure joy or maintenance meant to dislodge suckerfish or other pests attached to their bellies, he didn't know. But it was questions like this Eddie spent endless time pondering.

He did much of his wandering alone drawn on by his own curiosity. He never tired of exploring the tidal flats that were covered and uncovered by each changing cycle. As the tide went out, pools were left where small tropical fish would be trapped. He often took a quart jar with him on his expeditions. He'd fill it with salt water and catch sea horses, damsels, clown fish or whatever he could find to bring home. Next morning, having depleted the oxygen in their small glass prison, they were usually floating belly up, their brilliant rainbow colors faded in death to a dull gray. Undeterred, he would set out again and again, his jar held ready at his side, like a gunslinger looking for his next challenge.

These same mud flats, when above water, harbored large colonies of fiddler crabs, thousands at times, whose sole occupation was rolling up as many perfectly round mud balls as possible before the incoming waves washed away the product of all their labor. Eddie failed to understand the purpose of this activity. He found it a great mystery that the tiny creatures would continue this hard work, which was absolutely necessary to their survival, without reward.

When Eddie was older, he played hooky from school as often as he dared to, to fish or simply to wile away the day gazing into the ever-changing kaleidoscope of the shallows. At the bay front, he would often encounter Cristobal, an old Bahamian who had lost one leg in a dynamite explosion. It was Cristobal who taught him how to shell conchs. Using a hammer and screwdriver to break a small hole near the pointed end of the shell, the old fisherman showed him the strip of sinewy tissue that held the snail's body deep inside. Then he exchanged the hammer and screwdriver for a knife with a narrow, curved blade. Slipping it into the knocked-out hole, he sliced the muscle free from its anchor then jabbed the instrument into the mouth of the shell dragging the slick creature out where it dropped into his bucket with a plop. When the pail was full, the old man would hobble off on his peg leg to sell the conch meat to an upscale eatery and peddle his burlap sack filled with pearly pink shells to several of the local souvenir shops.

Eddie often spent the afternoons walking around the elegant estates that lined the bay. He was always on the lookout for packs of vicious dogs that had been left to roam the frontage of the estates' beautifully manicured gardens to keep intruders like him off the premises. Villa Vizcaya, his favorite place to wander, was a replica of an Italian Renaissance villa with rear grounds that included a salt-water pool and Romanesque pillared barge. To reach his special spot, he had to carefully work his way around the many barbed-wire entanglements placed meticulously by the owner to keep strangers off the property. It was just there, right below the coral rock seawall in four or five feet of water, that the shallow sea floor sparkled like a colorful Persian carpet with myriad yellow and purple sponges, small brain coral and delicate red sea fans that gently waved in the current. He lingered to watch the rainbow-colored parrotfish that swam among them nibbling at their frilly edges. Frequently, he would see the solitary fin of a shark cut through the water as it circled the nearby shallows looking for dinner.

Those protected coastal waters that enthralled Eddie and served up bounties for predatory fish also provided a perfect ingress for other opportunists. The fast boats of bootleggers cruised there with the same regularity as the sharks. Like them, they were busiest after dark, crisscrossing the channels between the Bahamas and the Florida coast bringing in the contraband that supplied the homes with manicured lawns. These waters were a training ground where a careful observer could discover many things. The lessons Eddie learned there were to his mind much more interesting than the boring facts he was required to memorize in a stuffy classroom.

Two

As might be expected in a city filled with sinful enticements, the Boyds had sought to shelter their only child from the rough edges of life by enrolling Eddie in a good Catholic school. It was their belief that the sisters and priests of St. Joseph would take on the responsibility for which they had scant time and little interest. The only thing accomplished by inserting Eddie into a place of goodness and discipline was the false sense of security they achieved for themselves.

Upon entering his teenage years, Eddie was not what would have been described as a social success. He wasn't athletic, and although his parents sent him to cotillion, his total lack of rhythm made him a complete failure as a dancer. The only skill he had thus far demonstrated was fishing, an ability he had honed to perfection while hanging around the jetties with his closest school friend Jim Flanagan.

Although Anne Boyd felt that her family was a social notch above the Flanagans, the two did attend mass together each Sunday at St. Joseph's. Other than both being Irish and Catholic, the Flanagans and the Boyds had little in common. Jim and Eddie had known each other as long as either could remember. They were salt and pepper.

Eddie was shy and serious. Too tall for his skinny frame, he tried to disguise his gangly appearance by affecting a casual slouch. His shock of unruly black hair defied every attempt to slick it back in the current style—or in any style at all.

Jim was in many ways Eddie's exact opposite. He was only five feet five and compact. Had it not been for his easy Irish charm, he might have been teased about his short stature or become a target for bullies. But Jim possessed natural wit and a roguish smile and had an uncanny ability to dance like Fred Astaire. These qualities made him a great hit with girls. Maybe it was their giggling, open admiration that impressed the other boys. At any rate, he was popular with everyone and at ease in a way that Eddie envied. Despite Eddie's grudging acquiescence to Jim's efforts to pull him along to soirees and social events, Eddie preferred to remain in the background daydreaming about shipwrecks and treasure or thinking about fishing.

Jim's parents were a busy, smiling couple that ran a dry cleaner, and during business hours they were rarely home. Most days, Eddie and Jim would come directly from school to Eddie's house, where the cupboard was always stocked with fresh bread and homemade jelly. Afterward, they headed outside to roam the streets or fish until it was dark.

Their neighborhood was only a few blocks from the bay. Every house had at least one mango tree, and during late spring and early summer, the yards were covered with rotting fruit. He and Jim waged wars against other neighbor kids, often arriving home covered in yellow mush. Their clothing and skin would be soaked with the sticky splatter of fruit. At Eddie's house, the scene typically elicited reprimands as his mother handed him over to their maid Beatrice, who, after a great deal of frowning and clucking, somehow managed to remove the orange stains.

When mango season was over, their favorite weapons were the plentiful land crabs. They weren't the tiny variety of crab that scuttled about on the rocks along the shoreline and jetties. These were bright blue, armored giants whose bodies spanned five to six inches across.

When on the move, they stood nearly six inches high. Every yard was pockmarked with the holes they perpetually dug. Like infantry, they maneuvered in groups. These crab platoons were forever marching back and forth from one side of the street or sidewalk to the other on mysterious missions. When the mood struck, Jim and Eddie would run along side one, grab him by a couple of legs, and fling him at a target. A hit around the ankles of an opponent would usually break the crab's shell and send a splash of juicy entrails over the screaming victim.

The boys usually emerged from battle covered in crab innards but otherwise unscathed. One awful day, Eddie was barefoot when he took a direct hit. When the crab didn't splatter, it locked its giant claw around his big toe. Eddie managed to shake the creature off, but the massive amputated claw remained firmly attached to his foot. Before long, Eddie's toe had turned the same purplish-blue color as the pincer. He hopped around laughing like a maniac trying to disguise his pain and the tears streaking down his cheeks. Although he attempted a display of dogged bravado, shouting his indignation and insisting that he was fine, he was secretly thankful when Jim left to go fetch Mrs. Boyd. She arrived with a hammer and pliers, and after some prying, broke the pincer loose. Following the episode, Eddie's toe and his ego were seriously bruised, and he was crab-shy for weeks.

The things he and Jim shared most were their love of fishing and the water. From the time they were little, they knew the location of and had fished every good spot within ten miles of their houses. Nearly every day after school, they'd throw their gear into their bicycle baskets and head to one of these spots. There, they'd eat their jelly sandwiches, fish and spin endless pipe dreams of a life together at sea.

Both were voracious readers who had read and reread each and every novel by authors Nordoff and Hall who wrote stories set in Polynesia.

The writers' descriptions of an unspoiled South-Sea paradise populated by beautiful, bare-breasted women and feather-crested warriors ignited their imagination and longing for adventure. Their most discussed and mulled-over scheme was a sketchy plan to build a boat and sail it to Tahiti. There, they planned to beach comb and live off what the land and sea provided, never to return home.

Compared to the starchy demeanor of the Boyd family, the easy-going atmosphere of Jim's home was a source of envy for Eddie as was the irrepressible warmth and optimism of the big Greek clan, the Mouskouris, who were the Boyd's next-door neighbors. The Mouskouri family had recently emigrated from Greece. They'd come to Miami where they opened a small neighborhood fish market. Although George Mouskouri, like so many recently arrived immigrants, had happily embraced the American dream of private ownership, he had never lost his love of the sea. Soon after reaching the shores of his new land, George had sent for his two brothers Peter and Nikolas, who had followed him with their families and now lived nearby. The brothers fished for a living, and each day's catch provided the family's market with fresh seafood. When the extended family gathered around the dining table and talked about the days in Greece before coming to America, George's eyes sometimes welled with emotion.

Eddie had spent many nights in their noisy kitchen eating and listening to George's tales about the old country where his family had been sponge divers. The vivid descriptions of crystal waters and shipwreck-strewn reefs just waiting to be explored added vivid colors to the canvas of Eddie's imagination and piqued his longing for adventure.

George and his wife Sophia had a large brood, which seemed to include a new member nearly every year. They trained the oldest children to watch the younger ones so that during busy periods at the market, Sophia, with the newest baby at her breast, could help George behind the counter. They weren't particular about school attendance either, and day and night there were usually children around the house. Their home had two stories and a flat roof that provided a perfect platform for star gazing or watching slow-moving clouds change shape. When there were no adults around, Eddie would sometimes seek out the eldest boy Peter, who was his age, for a game of cribbage. Like all the members of the Mouskouri family, Peter had a mop of curly black hair, dark eyes and swarthy Mediterranean good looks. Smart and quick to laugh, he was George's obvious favorite. Eddie was unabashedly envious, secretly wishing he and his father shared that sort of bond.

The Mouskouris' kitchen was the hub of the house, and Sophia, who loved to cook and eat, spent most of her time there when she was not assisting George at the market. Whenever Eddie spoke about Sophia at home, his mother would roll her eyes in obvious derision. In her opinion, Sophia was a little too plump for pretty, and Anne ridiculed her broken English. This angered Eddie. To him, Sophia's plumpness was the sure sign of a woman who loved her home and family. He sensed the real reason for his mother's resentment was that Sophia possessed all those qualities of warmth and domesticity that she herself lacked.

At the Boyd home, it was Beatrice who did most of the cooking. Beatrice had come to them when she was just a girl. When her mother, a seamstress who had sewn for a friend of Anne's, became ill, Eddie's mother took Beatrice in and gave her room and board and a meager salary in exchange for her services as maid, cook, and nursemaid to little Eddie. She had been with them ever since. She was, in fact, only ten years older than Eddie. She was sweet-natured and fiercely loyal.

In the Boyd home, it was Beatrice's calmness that provided a welcome counter-balance to the high-strung temperament of Eddie's mother. Even if Beatrice's culinary abilities had been vast, her menus were limited by the bland and unimaginative tastes of Eddie's parents, who preferred their meals boiled and overcooked. Corned beef and cabbage, chicken and dumplings and, on Fridays, poached fish and beets were the staple diet.

In contrast, every night at the Mouskouris' house, the table brimmed with rich food that Eddie found exotic and delicious. The scent of cinnamon, cloves, mint, oregano, thyme, and the pungent fragrance of lamb or fish announced each evening's mouth-watering fare.

Eddie felt warm and content simply sitting and watching Sophia move about the kitchen. She was gentle and feminine in some indefinable way that his mother wasn't. When she crossed from the stove to the table carrying steaming moussaka or a plate piled high with baklava, her bobbing golden earrings caught the light and her full hips swayed beneath the flowered housedresses she favored. Her golden skin and deep black eyes defined for Eddie his first notion of female beauty.

"Sit, eat," she would insist, waving a hand at Eddie. "You too skinny, you know? You need some meat on your bones!" And he often did, happily allowing himself to remain enveloped for a little longer in the comfortable glow of their big, happy family, the warmth punctuated by an occasional hug from Sophia.

Turning to him one night at dinner, George spoke about his homeland, a staccato finger tapping out bullet points on the table top. "Eddie, never here do you see water so clear like diamond, like in Greece!" He pointed to the heavens. "When I was just small boy, I can dive fifty, maybe sixty feet down. One time, I am diving in a big shipwreck, maybe fifteen hundred year old. Ship is carrying great load of the statues, amphora full of wine, olive oil. I am looking for something small, light enough to bring up with me. In sand, I see something gold, shiny. Just then, I feel the big rope around my ankle. But isn't rope. Is big *chtopadi*—octopus you call it—with head huge like watermelon, arms maybe eight feet long, and he has my leg! He's hiding in big broken amphora and he try to pull me inside. Now, I am running out of air fast. I don't know what to do."

"What, Mr. Mouskouri? What did you do?" Eddie asked, pinned to his chair by excitement.

"Well, I am one very lucky fellow, I tell you! I have always the knife strap to my leg. I grab and begin to cut. But is not easy, you know? I think I am sure going to drown. Octopus leg is very hard, all muscle. I cut and cut, and finally, off go the leg. I begin to kick, up, up, but my air is gone, and I can't kick no more. I am many feet below surface, and just when I know I am going to die, Niko he swim down to me and pull me up. How you like that!"

"How did you stay down so long?" asked Eddie, clearly impressed.

"The sponge diver must learn special way to breathe. I teach you?" George's offer dangled there.

"Would you?" Eddie couldn't believe it.

"Sure!" George said. "I am also lucky what I find that day. It was very fine cup. All gold, with the athletes carved on the side. I sell to big art dealer in Athens. With the money, we come to America. Here we can do anything!" He spread his arms in a grand gesture and grinned broadly.

Eddie looked up to see Sophia gazing at George with pure adoration. He had often caught George looking at her the same way. Eddie had never seen his mother and father look at each other like that. After the stories at the end of the evening meal, Eddie pitched in with the other children clearing off the table. Standing at the sink hip to hip with Sophia, he determined someday to have a family like this one.

*   *   *

Ed met Diana's gaze with a piercing glance and a slightly raised brow. His eyes suddenly clouded over.

"Of course all that was before I met Manny. I didn't know then how much things were about to change."

Diana was silent. She scanned his face, her gaze dropping to the blunted thumb he unconsciously drew along the edge of the china coffee cup. When he looked up and caught her staring at him, an unexpected fear rose in his throat. He nervously looked down at his hands and, as if talking to himself said softly, "Nothing was the same after that."

THREE

One fall afternoon not long after that evening at Peter's, the sun had dropped to just above the tree line, and Eddie knew exactly where the fish would be biting. Jim had to help his mother put up wall paper in the kitchen and couldn't come along, so he had grabbed his pole and headed for one of his special places about half-an-hour's walk from his house.

A small inlet protected by two narrow fingers of mangrove hammock provided a shady shelter where large numbers of medium-sized snapper and grunt sought refuge from the hot mid-day sun. It was just about the time of day they would begin moving out of the shadows and swimming out toward the middle of the inlet. As they became more active, they began feeding, and he could almost always catch something at about this hour. He baited his hook and cast his line toward a shady spot near a tangle of mangrove roots across the inlet and slowly began reeling his line back in.

In the shallows near where he stood, a Jesus bug tiptoed across the quicksilver mirror of water. With its widespread, hair-covered back legs and long feet, the bug could perform the impossible feat of walking on water. Although the creature couldn't see through his own reflection to the bottom, his delicate sense organs could detect the tiniest disturbance of the water molecules on the surface. When a movement sent ripples across his shiny dance floor, the Jesus bug darted to it, ready to grab his lunch. This time, though, rather than the mosquito wriggler he expected, he encountered the toothy beak of a hungry needlefish. In a flash, the Jesus bug disappeared. The ripples subsided, and in seconds the surface was as calm as it had been before, minus the Jesus bug. It was gone, as if it had never been there at all.

After five or ten minutes had passed without a bite, Eddie decided to move on to another spot. He worked his way up one finger of the hammock until he found another promising location. A foot or two back in the trees, the thick thatch of mangrove roots formed a seat of sorts where he could sit comfortably while he waited for a bite. On his way there, he had snared some fiddler crabs to use as bait and tied them in a piece of old dishtowel. Now he baited his hook with one that still had enough life left to dance a bit on the bottom. He hoped its activity would entice a nice fat snapper. The sound of low voices and the crunch of a boat bottom scraping against gravel broke his concentration. The rumble of an approaching vehicle followed within seconds.

Curious, he slithered through the dense leaves and cautiously peered out to identify the source of the sounds. On the other side of the small inlet where he was fishing, a wider inlet sheltered a thirty or forty-yard stretch of open beach. There, no more than fifteen yards from where Eddie hid, he could see a huge, burly man whose face in profile was completely flat; where a nose should have been there was only the hint of a bump just above his top lip. From the man's position on the shore, he was issuing orders to two others. They waded back and forth in the ankle deep water unloading wooden crates from the boat and transferring them into the cargo bay of a panel truck backed up to the water's edge. At a closer glance, Eddie noticed that the big man supervising the operation looked peculiarly out of place. He was too well dressed to be out here walking around in the seaweed and tide-wash on a hot, humid day. He wore a checkered suit with wide shoulders and lapels that were the latest fashion, a colorful leaf-patterned tie and wide yellow suspenders, and his thick neck bulged out over the too-tight collar of his shirt. His flushed face ran with sweat.

When a sudden shift of the boat sent a ripple of brownish water over the big man's shoes, he cursed and jumped back from the water's edge. He yelled at the driver of the boat, as if it had been his fault. He was a wiry man with a wind-blown thatch of red hair and sunburned skin.

"Christ!" he blurted out, "Look out, can't ya, Alderman? Look at my shoes! I gotta be at Salvatore's by nine, and the shoeshine stand will be closed by the time I get back. Geez!"

He moved with surprising agility for a man his size. Pulling a handkerchief from his breast pocket, he angrily dabbed one of his soiled brown and white wingtips.

"Hey, you should take off those fancy shoes, Manny. How you expect them to stay clean walking around in dirty water and gull shit?" Alderman shot back.

A mischievous grin lit up the red-haired man's face exposing big, square teeth the size of Chiclets with a wide space between the two front ones. Alderman continued to push.

"What, You got a hot date, Manny? Hell, they look good enough for a broad," he said.

"No," Manny glared back and cursed under his breath.

Sudden comprehension flashed across Alderman's face.

"Ahhhh, you're gonna meet with the boss, huh," he stated matter-of-factly, shaking his head. Manny shot Alderman a look followed by a few seconds of silence that clearly signaled he should shut up.

Eddie studied Manny curiously. While he paced back and forth keeping a close watch on the activities of the men unloading the boat, his eyes frequently darted back out into the bay scanning the open water. He spoke to the men with authority but kept his voice low. After a few minutes, Alderman hopped over the side to wade through the shallow water and floating clumps of Sargasso weed toward where Manny was standing beyond the water's edge. They conversed softly with each other for a few moments. Eddie strained to catch what they were saying.

"As soon as you unload this, I'm heading straight back to Bimini for another pick-up. Real prime stuff next time." Alderman spoke reconcilably.

"When should we look for you again?" the big man asked.

"On Friday afternoon. Remember, though, high tide will be later by then. Be sure you check the charts."

Manny looked back a bit wearily. "Well, I hope it's not too late. I have some other business."

They continued to talk while the others stacked another dozen rough wooden crates stenciled with the word *Bananas* into the back of the vehicle.

When they finished transferring the boxes into the vehicle, all but Alderman climbed in. The engine sputtered to life, and the truck, now so loaded it barely cleared the rocky hump in the path between the wheel ruts, turned around and bounced slowly back down the sand and coquina path. When it was out of sight, Eddie scrambled out of the underbrush in time to see the boat and its lone occupant speed off toward the channel buoys. As he watched them disappear into the distance, he wondered where this mysterious cargo was headed. He was less curious about the contents of the cases; he was pretty certain they didn't contain bananas. It wasn't the cargo but the conversation that captured his interest. On Monday, everything closed by nine. Why would the big man say he had business at Salvatore's at that hour?

When the boat and truck were gone, he went back to fishing. But his thoughts were now occupied with the truck and its destination, and after a few minutes he packed up his tackle and started home. The sun was hovering over the low banks of purple clouds, bathing everything in the brief golden glow that occurs before dusk, when the light and the atmosphere are just right. Eddie always found this particular time of day magical and stopped whatever he was doing to watch until the moment was gone and darkness fell; this evening he didn't even notice. Instead, he hurried quickly toward his destination, Alderman's words still with him as he pondered the other bounties that floated in on the incoming tide.

Four

Later that night, the light over the door of Salvatore's Trattoria went out on time at 9:00 P.M. Inside, a waiter wiped his hands on his apron and leaned across a table at the front window to flip the OPEN sign to CLOSED.

At 9:10, a Cadillac pulled up in front. The driver got out and stepped around to open the door for the two occupants in the back seat. A short, stocky man wearing a white suit climbed out followed by a thin, ferret-faced companion. When they had exited, the third occupant, a hulking figure with a boxer's powerful build, emerged from the front passenger seat. He signaled the driver to park the car down a side street on the next block and wait for them.

*   *   *

Eddie lay with his eyes closed quietly waiting to hear the snap of his door closing. As soon as his mother bid him goodnight and shut the door to his room, he listened to her footsteps fading down the hall. He counted slowly to twenty before he slipped out of bed and softly pulled the chair away from his school desk to a position under the window. At Eddie's age, his lankiness often made him clumsy, but his height could be an advantage. Tonight it was. Stepping up silently, he eased the window up. He jack-knifed his body into the opening. Unfolding his long legs outside, he dropped to the ground and slipped out into the night.

Hurrying along the darkened streets toward his objective, he arrived just after nine. He positioned himself in the shadows on the side of a building across the street from Salvatore's just in time to see the car pull up and its occupants emerge. From his hiding place, Eddie clearly recognized the huge man's silhouette.

He watched as the three entered the empty establishment, exchanged a few words with the waiter and were shown to a table at the rear of the room. Eddie stealthily crossed the street and slid into the alley behind the restaurant. There, he gingerly moved an up-ended trashcan under a high open window. Cautiously, he climbed up and peaked inside. He had a clear view of the tabletop. Three places were set, wine glasses and a full bottle of Chianti sat at the fourth empty spot. As soon as they were seated, the proprietor hurried out from the kitchen. He gave a small bow as he reached the table. From the position directly under his perch, Eddie saw a white-sleeved hand extend toward the waiter, who kissed it. The two exchanged a few words in the soft dialect of southern Italy. The waiter poured the wine with a kind of slow reverence and set a glass before each of the three before he bustled back to the kitchen, leaving its door to flap wildly back and forth sending rich aromas of garlic and basil out through the window. In a few minutes he was back with plates of antipasti. He set the colorful meats and pickles on the table, bowing again with the same reverence as when he'd poured the wine. Only after he returned to the kitchen, did the diners begin to speak with each other. Eddie's position placed him too directly over the tabletop to see all of them, but he could hear well enough.

"After we eat, there's a matter—a problem, if you will—we need you to take care of," he heard the white-suited man say to the big man at his right. He spoke softly and slowly, as if measuring his words with great care. Eddie noticed a trace of emotion in his tone that resembled regret.

"Marco can no longer be trusted. I have it on good authority, one I can believe like my own two eyes," he continued.

He paused when the waiter reappeared, allowing him to place the next course of spaghetti marinara with mussels before them and retreat back into the kitchen before continuing. Eddie could see the white-sleeved hand dig a mussel from its shell and swirl it in sauce. After the bite, he continued.

"You know what that means. A dog that rolls in shit will leave a trail of stink that leads right back to its own bed. We can't afford that. So tonight I want you to take Marco to see that new stripper down at the Gulf Breeze Club. She goes on at eleven. That's a nice last meal don't you think? Here," he said, reaching into his pocket. Eddie saw the manicured hands holding a wad of bills as he peeled a hundred from the bulging roll and handed it across to Manny. "And then, drop him off at the pier."

"I'll show him a good time," Manny's voice came back.

Other than the small man refusing a second glass of wine, they finished their meal in silence. Eddie didn't understand the "problem" mentioned, but he was pretty sure it wasn't good for Marco.

Eddie wished he looked older. The strip club didn't have windows, and he knew he wouldn't be allowed inside. He remained in his hiding place until Salvatore escorted the trio out and locked the door behind them. The owner turned back to the table, having dismissed the waiter earlier, and began to clear away the dishes. From under one of them, he plucked a fifty-dollar bill. Eddie saw him slip it into his apron pocket with a smile that said it was well worth entertaining these men after closing time.

When Salvatore disappeared with the last of the plates, Eddie gingerly lowered himself from his position so as not to rattle the metal can under him and cautiously tiptoed out of the alley toward home. It was well past 10:30 when the owner left for the night, and by then Eddie was back in his room and fast asleep.

*   *   *

The stage at the Gulf Breeze was in total darkness except for a blue spotlight illuminating a narrow, ceiling-to-floor swag of black velvet that hung down on the left side of the stage. A tall blonde, entirely naked but for tiny sequined pasties and a g-string no wider than thin twine, was straddling the curtain with her legs and grinding her hips in time to the rhythm of Ravel's *Bolero*. The tempo increased and she spread her legs wider, pulling the soft curtain back and forth against her crotch and rubbing it on her breasts. She began to moan as she tossed her head from side to side, and then she leaned backwards, sending her long hair flying back and forth across her face like a whip. She caught and released strands of it provocatively from the corners of her open mouth as she raised and lowered her chin in rhythm to the pounding music. Her hips were now pumping fast, and on the last note of the music's blaring crescendo of wailing horns and crashing cymbals, the stage went black. Marco clapped wildly and whistled.

"She's something, ain't she?" he said, and jabbed his companion in the ribs.

After the first performance, they had had drinks at the bar while they waited for the second show to begin.

Marco downed several, laughing and grabbing at the waitress in his stupor. The stripper in the second show was a brunette with little talent but bigger breasts.

It was after one o'clock when Marco weaved his way through the tables and out onto the warm pavement heading for the parked car. Manny followed, guiding him. By this time, Marco was so unsteady on his feet that Manny had to practically shove him into the front seat.

"It's hot, Marco," he said, after getting behind the wheel. "Crank that window down, okay?"

The warm breeze felt good. In five minutes, Marco was asleep and snoring softly, his head slumped forward on his chest.

Manny drove slowly taking care not to make any fast turns or stops. As they neared the docks, the traffic thinned until the streets became deserted. No one came to this area at night. Except for the one weak bulb that illuminated the door of a large warehouse and whatever moonlight was available, the area was dark. The big man guided the car toward a boat ramp next to one of the piers and let the car crawl to a stop. He reached under the seat and withdrew a pistol.

He looked at Marco's drooping head. He was in a dead stupor. When he raised the gun to Marco's temple and fired, most of the blood and brain matter sprayed out through the open window, clearing the door by a few feet. He was glad he had the foresight to have Marco roll down the window.

He got out, went around to the other side of the car and opened the door. Marco's accommodating body fell out heavily and rolled most of the way down the sloping ramp so that the big man had to nudge it only the last foot or two before it settled into the water. For a moment, the body bobbed in the shallow waves lapping up the slope. Finally, it began to drift out toward deeper water. The big man stood quietly watching Marco's spread-eagle form slowly recede from the shore until his shape was no more than a small, black, emptiness on a sea of reflected stars.

He walked back to the car, careful to avoid the glistening black puddle on the pavement. Before getting in, he inspected the open passenger door closely. Taking out his handkerchief, he wiped a dark patch above the door handle. He carefully refolded the white cloth and was about to put the stained material back in his pocket when he glanced down at his feet.

"Damn," he growled under his breath. Several stray drops of blood dotted the white leather top of his wingtip shoe. He spat on a clean patch of cloth and rubbed hard until they disappeared.

When he turned to leave, the Manny checked his watch. If he hurried, he might make it back to the Gulf Breeze in time to see the end of the last show when the blonde would be on again. Marco had been right, he thought. She really was something.

*   *   *

It was just after midnight when the taxi glided silently up to the curb and then slid to a stop in front of a two-story house on Bayshore Drive. The windows were all dark except for a small curtained square next to the front door where a dim light glowed. A shadow passed briefly in front of it, and then the light went out leaving the interior in complete darkness.

A moment later, the front door swung open. Three figures emerged and stood for a second silhouetted against the pale stucco of the porch wall. An observer would easily have identified the forms as those of a woman and two children, the smaller one clutching an animal-shaped bundle in one arm. The woman paused to close and lock the door and then struggled down the walk lugging a large suitcase. She quietly urged her two small charges toward the waiting vehicle.

The driver hurried out, took the bulky bag from her and hoisted it into the back while the three passengers climbed into the rear seat.

"Shh," the woman murmured, pulling the smaller child's head to her bosom. "I told you. We have to. You'll help Mommy, won't you? It'll be all right, you'll see." Muffled under her arm, the child continued to sob. The woman checked the three tickets to Chicago in her handbag. "Please hurry," she ordered the driver, "we have a train to catch."

He slammed the rear door then slipped back behind the wheel. He slowly backed the automobile around and moved off in the same direction from which he had come. Soon the taillights faded into the darkness and disappeared in the moonless night. In less than two minutes, the cab had come and gone leaving only the empty house as silent witness to its occupants' hasty departure.

*   *   *

Two mornings later, Eddie lay sprawled on the floor with the newspaper spread out in front of him. He had never before shown more than a passing interest in anything but the sports page and the funnies, but since his recent encounters at the inlet and Salvatore's, he had suddenly developed an intense fascination with the news sections.

One front-page story piqued his interest. *Bootleggers Have Last Laugh*. He scanned the article hoping to learn more about this apparently booming business. The article had charged Sheriff "Pogy

Bill" Williams with supervising rumrunners' activities and thereby controlling bootlegging in Okeechobee, a county just north of Miami. The rest of the article provided few details but much speculation from "an anonymous but reliable source". Although bootlegging was widespread in those days of prohibition, Eddie was still naïve enough to be surprised that an official elected to uphold the law was actually profiting from and running an illegal activity.

He turned the page. The headline and photo at the top of page two caused him to draw in a sharp breath. *Body Washes Up On Haulover Beach*. He read on.

> *The body of a man was found early Wednesday morning at Baker's Haulover by two vacationers, Mr. and Mrs. Alfred J. Levy from Trenton, New Jersey. The police have identified the body as that of Marco Scalone, a known mobster with connections to Alphonse Capone. The Dade County coroner verified that Scalone was killed by a single gunshot to the head. Police theorize that his murder was another mob hit.*

In the accompanying photo, a sheet-draped form lay sprawled atop a pile of seaweed at the high tide line near the feet of two policemen and an emotionally shaken Mr. Levy, who pointed toward the mound.

*   *   *

The coffee pot was empty, and the clock over the stove read 8:30 A.M. Sunlight now streamed through the kitchen windows.

"My God, Dad, that's a scene right out of a movie," Diana said in a hushed voice. "Weren't you scared?"

"The mob was everywhere in those days," he said waving his hand as if shooing a fly. "Everyone knew them. To the rest of us they were just part of the community. Jim and I went to school with their kids."

"What if they'd caught you spying?"

He removed his glasses, rubbed his eyes and looked away. "I'm feeling kind of tired now. I think I could go back to sleep for a while."

Diana nodded agreement but flashed him a concerned look, suddenly aware just how frail he was.

"I have a hair appointment in Coconut Grove this morning," she said, "but I want to hear the rest of the story. Why don't you go back to sleep while I'm out, and we'll talk more later on." She smiled, patting his hand.

Nodding, he slid his chair back from the table and shuffled off to his bedroom. He stretched out on top of the covers, and staring up at the patchwork of leafy shadows spread across the ceiling, he realized he *was* tired. That much was true. The real reason he'd broken off his narrative, though, was Diana. Her expression at hearing about Marco had been one of shock. What if he told her the rest of the story? He didn't want to chance driving her away when they'd only just begun to know each other. Especially not after he'd quietly admitted to himself that maybe he needed her too.

He closed his eyes. Manny. How could he explain Manny to someone with no inkling what those days were like? But now he'd started the story, and going forward seemed the only way. To do otherwise would destroy the fragile bridge of honesty he and Diana had begun to build. But he knew, too, that to continue would definitely test its strength.

FIVE

Later that night, seated side by side on the porch swing, Diana gently prodded, "So, tell me more, Dad. You really knew criminals?"

"Yes, I knew a few . . . some of their families," he stumbled. "You have to remember, it was a peculiar time. Prohibition was a stupid and futile attempt to legislate morality. I mean, if you take away something that's enjoyable and make it illegal people will want it all the more. Most of the so-called criminals just considered themselves savvy businessmen who were providing something everyone wanted, even if it was illegal like marijuana is today. Sure, some of them like Al Capone were unscrupulous and way too powerful. Usually, though, the consumers didn't care how the business was run as long as the booze kept flowing."

It was a strange time; he remembered it as if it were yesterday.

*　　　*　　　*

At almost sixteen, he was still an inexperienced teenager, but even as sheltered as he had been, he knew members of the underworld and their families were a part of Miami society. Ironically, it was in the safe environment of St. Joseph's school that he had first become acquainted with one of them. On the day of the newcomer's arrival, Sister Pauline had introduced him to the class.

Behind her back, the students referred to Sister Pauline as "The Stick" because she carried a baton to whack the hands of anyone who might be up to something. She also had an inscrutable expression that she kept for certain occasions, an uncanny way of smoothing out her features until her face was as flat as a flounder with no lines to read between. She set her face before speaking.

"This is Albert Francis Capone, class," she announced. "His father recently bought Delaney's Furniture Movers, and now he has moved his family from Chicago to Miami. I know you will all welcome him to St. Joseph's."

"Yeah, sure," someone in the back of the room whispered. "Only my father says the crates in his delivery trucks aren't full of furniture." Someone else tittered, but Sister quickly stared the guilty party down. Again silence reigned. No one wanted to incur the wrath of The Stick or the sting that accompanied her flying whip on his or her outstretched palms.

Each day Sonny was driven across the causeway to school by Frank, a tall, lanky man in his father's employ. His sole business, it appeared, was to take Sonny up to his classroom in the morning and to pick him up at the last bell.

Sonny's chauffeur carried a .45 automatic in his hip pocket, the handle making a prominent bulge under his jacket. After dropping Sonny off at school, Frank would spend his day hanging out in the little sundry shop across from the school entrance where many students had lunch. He also spent hours leaning against the car talking to the cop on the beat.

The Cadillac that Frank drove was a brand new, two-tone black and tan seven passenger sedan. On the day Sonny had first been enrolled, the kids all leaned out the window to gawk and take bets on who at St. Joseph's might own such a magnificent machine. It had white-wall tires on wired wheels and sported bumper-mounted driving lamps rather than the old-style ones mounted on the cowl. Sonny told someone his father had had it specially equipped with bulletproof glass, and that fully equipped, it had cost over $3,000.

At exactly five minutes to three every day, Frank would saunter back to the no parking zone where he had left the car parked all day and collect Sonny for the return trip home. Frank never smiled. While the opportunity to ride in the latest model Caddy equipped with all the newest gadgets made Sonny the envy of all, Eddie couldn't help feeling sorry for him having to endure Frank's sullen stare twice a day. He wondered if this was all Frank did to earn his money. Maybe that was the reason he had a constant scowl. Being a professional chauffeur for a kid wasn't the kind of job a person could really brag about.

Except for Sonny, the other students at St. Joseph's were pretty ordinary. Just like Eddie, they were the children of mostly middle class families who wanted the strict environment of a Catholic school to keep their kids in line. And the nuns and priests took their jobs very seriously.

By the time Eddie was about to enter high school, the nuns began to find him a challenge. Fortunately, Jesuit priests, who had a better grip on teenage boys, taught the high school classes. One, in particular, kept Eddie under his watchful gaze. This was Father Horka. Unlike most priests, he was young and had a sense of humor. He didn't look like any priest Eddie had ever seen, either. He was tall and muscular with curly, black hair and a face that the girls at the school described as dreamy. It was rumored that he had played football for Notre Dame; in fact, when he wasn't wearing his vestments, he looked more like an athlete than a priest. But when the Great War broke out, he had joined the Army and been sent to France.

After only six months at the front, he was hit by a German bullet and sent home with a bronze star and a bad limp—a terrible tragedy for a football star, everyone said. The severity of his injury required him to spend months recuperating in a military hospital. The outward sign of his injury was the limp, but the bullet had damaged more than his athletic career. When he returned home, he felt it only fair that he break off his engagement to his college sweetheart.

Soon after, he had joined the priesthood. Still, he had a sense of humor, and occasionally he would even take part in a dice game with the boys. Although he strictly forbade gambling for money, he would allow the boys to put up their promise of chores in exchange for his special dispensation from a homework assignment.

In spite of Father Horka's influence, Eddie had just entered into that stage of adolescence where mysterious forces pulled at him. Most obvious and troubling were the constant thoughts of sex that seemed to rear up at the most inopportune times. At the very least, those occasions were the source of embarrassment to him; at the worst, they convinced him that he would end up in hell if he didn't get himself under control. But he began to have other, more vague feelings that he had never experienced before and didn't have words to categorize. Sometimes when he was fishing or puttering around contentedly, a dark cloud would suddenly descend upon him, and the very next moment he'd be kicking at a log or slamming his fist into a nearby wall with an unfocused anger that he could neither anticipate nor control.

Those swings between euphoria and melancholy threw him off course like a compass needle in the presence of an invisible magnet. The uncertainty of these sudden mood changes kept him in a perpetual state of angst. He found himself itching to trade in the innocent preoccupations of childhood for the adventure and liberties of adulthood. Of course, liberty required some degree of financial independence, and as yet, he had none at all.

The small change he earned selling frog legs to Mouskouri's Market was kid stuff, hardly enough to produce a jingle in his pocket. He had already decided he didn't intend to spend the rest of his life living from hand to mouth like his parents did; consequently, poised at the doorway to perdition with one foot at the threshold, his every thought persistently returned to the mysterious boat he had seen and the articles he had read in the paper.

Monsignor Abernethy, the principal at St. Joseph's, frequently warned his charges that the road to Hell is as steep and smooth as a greased slide. If they weren't constantly on guard, he told the students, they'd soon find themselves tumbling down that slippery slope hanging on for dear life. The fear that this warning had always produced in Eddie was beginning to give way to an attitude of rebellion, and the flickering fires of hell were starting to look more and more like the twinkle of gold at the end of a rainbow.

PART TWO

Manny

Six

St. Joseph's was centrally located in downtown Miami and was surrounded by department stores and the numerous arcades, which occupied the ground floor of many of the downtown buildings. Eddie and Jim would occasionally slip out during lunch to these cool, busy tunnels and succumb to their dark allure, sometimes losing track of time and missing most of their afternoon classes. Lately, Eddie was finding it more difficult to fight the constant temptation to skip school altogether to roam there.

The arcades were like oases where pedestrians could leave the hot, noisy streets and enter another world of cool, quiet tunnels lined on both sides with dress, hat and cigar shops, shoeshine parlors, and rows of shiny slot machines. Gambling of every sort was wide open in those days, and on both sides of the arcades, spaced between the doorways of the shop entrances, the machines beckoned both shoppers and browsers.

Eddie received thirty cents for lunch each day but found that he could subsist on just two donuts and still have five nickels left for the slots. Usually, he spent most of it at the machines trying for the big payoff—two dollars for a nickel.

Bookies did business out of the backrooms of many respectable shops and protected themselves with regular payoffs to the police. It wasn't even necessary to go inside if you had credit with them. A phone call was enough to place a bet; for those unfortunate enough to let their bill get too high, however, the interest rate could be stiff—a broken arm or smashed kneecap.

After school one day when he and Jim were loitering in the arcades, Eddie led Jim toward a tobacconist shop located near the back entrance. As he had hoped they might, he spotted the big man he had seen directing the boat delivery at the inlet. He was having his shoes polished at the shoeshine stand next to The Pipe and Pouch. A hand-lettered sign on the wall above the chair advertised:

Best Shoeshine—15 cents Apples Free.

A brass spittoon sat on the floor on one side of the stand. On the other side, was a blue crockery bowl filled with apples, and the big man sat slouched comfortably in the chair finishing off a last mouthful of fruit. He pulled out his handkerchief and wiped away a stray drop of juice from his chin then refolded it neatly and replaced it in his pocket. When the shine was complete, he left, flipping a silver dollar to Junior, the grey-haired shoeshine boy.

"Did you see that?" Eddie whispered, amazed at the extravagance of an 85-cent tip.

"Yeah, Big Manny Silver," Jim replied. "And I know where he gets his money. Sonny told me Big Manny works for his father." They watched as Manny disappeared down the dim hallway and out the First Street exit.

Eddie began turning over in his mind what it might be like to be Sonny. He wondered if having people like Frank and Manny around all the time would be exciting. Fishing for more details from Jim, who seemed to know everything about everyone at school, Eddie said, "It must be nice having a powerful father and a chauffeur to boot."

"Maybe not," Jim observed solemnly. "Sonny said Frank's been with his family since about four years ago when some guys who worked for a rival gang in Chicago tried to kidnap him when he was just a little kid. That's one reason his father brought the family here. Even now, Sonny doesn't go anywhere without Frank. He can't even go off by himself to take a leak. Can you imagine that?" Jim asked.

Hearing that, Eddie decided he should take more of an interest in Sonny. He really was pretty nice, polite to the nuns, kind of quiet, and a better student than either Eddie or Jim. He made up his mind that first thing tomorrow he would stop laughing at the jokes some of the kids told about Sonny's father.

The next afternoon, just as Eddie was swallowing the last bite of his donut at the sandwich shop across from school, Manny's hulking figure darkened the doorway and approached the counter where Frank sat looking at a menu. Curious, Eddie decided to watch them to see what he could discover about their business. He sank back into a dim corner and pretended to thumb through one of his schoolbooks.

According to Jim, Big Manny was a lower-echelon member of Capone's organization. He did various jobs, but his usual one was to pick up the day's receipts from the many bookies, prostitutes and numbers sellers to make sure no one skimmed anything off the top. Eddie had seen him on a number of occasions since he'd found out who he was and had begun to study him closely.

Big Manny Silver was one of those men whose sheer size made it impossible for him to look neat. Although he wore obviously expensive, hand-tailored suits, his clothes were always slightly rumpled as if he had slept in them. Like many big men, he sweated profusely and constantly mopped his brow with a neatly folded handkerchief he kept in the inside breast pocket of his jacket.

Manny's most distinguishing features were his disfigured face and massive bulk. His nose had been badly broken and had healed almost completely flat. It twisted to the right at a severe angle just below the bridge. That face sat atop a bulky, six-foot five-inch body with the broad shoulders and thick neck of a wrestler. His frightening looks sometimes shocked little children, who often turned and stared at him after he had passed by.

Strangely, his appearance failed to have that effect on Eddie. Manny was big, but in a way that reminded him of a dancing bear he'd seen at the circus. As it toddled around its trainer at the end of its sturdy leash, it seemed more like a big poodle than a terrifying beast that could tear a person's arm off with one swipe of its razor claws.

Something else that struck Eddie as incongruous about Manny's appearance was his feet. They were unusually small for his size, probably no larger than an eight or nine. Standing, he looked like an upside-down triangle. But in spite of this seeming challenge to gravity, his movements, like those of the circus bear, were graceful; or maybe they just seemed so because you wouldn't expect grace from anyone his size.

Eddie had noticed, too, that Manny prided himself on his one neat physical feature. He must have had a huge wardrobe of shoes; Eddie had never seen him wear the same pair twice. Manny favored two-toned wingtips, which he kept immaculate. Trailing him around the arcades, Eddie had discovered that he had his shoes shined at Junior's stand every day.

On that particular day when Eddie encountered him in the sandwich shop, Big Manny was wearing a pale tan gabardine suit, wide maroon tie, brown and white shoes and was carrying a large alligator valise. Eddie watched him and Frank as they ate and talked. The two sat hunched over their blue-plate special lunches of steak and potatoes speaking in quiet voices. Eddie could tell it wasn't a friendly chat because the entire time they spoke they never looked directly at each other. Frank finished his steak, swiped the last of his fried potatoes through the lake of meat juice on his plate, then shoved them into his mouth and rose to leave. When he turned back and handed Manny an envelope, the big man quickly tucked it into his inside breast pocket. Eddie thought it would probably be a damp wad when he pulled it out.

Frank started walking toward the door but then stopped, turned abruptly, and pointing his finger at Manny, he spat out several angry sounding words. The clatter of dishes in the kitchen drowned out his voice making it impossible for Eddie to hear what he had said. Then, he spun on his heel and left. He didn't even pay for his lunch.

Big Manny opened his mouth as if to say something, but Frank was already gone. Manny stared after him. His face turned a deep shade of red, and he clenched and unclenched his jaw. He turned back to his unfinished lunch, but after a minute he angrily shoved his plate aside and handed the waitress a five-dollar bill. When she put his change down on the counter and headed toward the back with the dirty dishes, Manny didn't seem to notice. Leaving the money where she had placed it, he turned, grabbed up the valise and abruptly stormed out.

When he had gone, Eddie quickly swiped the bills off the counter and stuffed them into his pocket. Leaving the change for the waitress, he hurried out the door after him. Determined to see where Manny would go, Eddie followed at a discrete distance.

Eddie had been curious to learn how the numbers business worked. Now he had his opportunity to find out. When he saw Manny duck into a shop a few doors farther down the street, he decided to follow him inside. As Eddie was about to enter the doorway, a hand shot out, grabbed him by the throat, and pulled him into the room's dark interior. At the other end of the burly arm, Manny's frightening face glared down at him.

"What do you think you're doing following me?" he snarled. Not until he slightly loosened his grip, was Eddie able to choke out an answer.

"You forgot this on the lunch counter, Mr. Silver," Eddie stammered, thrusting the bills at him. "It's a lot of money."

"You know my name, huh. How'd you know that?" Big Manny demanded.

"I just heard. That's all." Eddie's blood pounded in his ears.

"Why didn't you just keep the money?" Manny said, plucking the crumpled bills from Eddie's hand.

Eddie thought he saw Manny's expression soften just a little, and that gave him the courage to go on.

"I was thinking . . . I mean hoping . . . you could use me to run errands . . . to earn a little something, you know. Yesterday I saw you at the shoeshine stand. I saw you give Junior an eighty-five cent tip, so you must make a lot of money. That's what I want to do," Eddie stammered in an avalanche of words that he poured out in a rush before he could lose his nerve.

Big Manny continued to stare at him as if closely inspecting a cockroach before swatting it with a newspaper. Finally, his face relaxed a bit more as he looked Eddie up and down.

"Shouldn't someone your age be in school?" Manny asked.

"Yeah, but I always have plenty of free time," he lied. "I know this part of town like the back of my hand. Maybe I could do odd jobs for you," Eddie hurriedly added.

For a long moment Manny stared at him but said nothing.

"Well since you've been tailing me for days, I guess you can follow me if you want to," Manny grumbled, "but don't be bothering me, or you're going to wish you'd stayed behind your mama's skirt." With that, he turned and started down the block.

Eddie stood in disbelief for a second. Was he kidding? Did letting him come along mean Manny was accepting his offer? He hadn't thought talking his way into a job would be this easy.

Manny was halfway down the block by the time Eddie looked up. In spite of a chorus of internal voices urging caution, he rushed after him. The length of Manny's stride made it necessary for Eddie to hop-step to catch up to him. With the resolution that he would keep his guard up, his eyes open and his mouth shut, Eddie quickly made his decision. His confidence was further bolstered by the thought that nothing bad could happen to him in broad daylight. And he refused to allow this opportunity to watch and learn slip through his fingers by being a coward, a Casper Milquetoast.

On his rounds that afternoon, Manny made many stops picking up paper bags and bulging white and brown envelopes that he stuffed into the leather valise. Since he ordered Eddie to wait for him outside each establishment, Eddie was disappointed not to be able to learn exactly how the transactions took place. What he did learn was that most of the stops were short and Manny was in and out in less than a minute.

Several times, though, Manny didn't return right away. Eddie wondered what was keeping him so long. He didn't have a watch, so when Manny had been inside for what seemed much longer than usual, Eddie began to count seconds. By the time he finally returned, Eddie calculated that nearly fifteen minutes had passed. When Manny rushed out in a huff, slamming the door behind him, he didn't say anything; his flushed face and the pinched scowl that forced his lips into a thin, white line told Eddie things hadn't gone well for someone.

They walked in silence for a few blocks. When they came to a frozen custard stand, Manny stopped. He pulled his handkerchief out and mopped at a rivulet of sweat that was crawling from his eyebrow and snaking down his cheek.

"I could use one of these, how about you?" Manny said, gesturing at the cart.

"Yeah," Eddie quickly agreed. He had been so excited and curious he hadn't realized how foot-weary and hot he was. Manny handed him a big cone of the drippy stuff, which had already begun to melt, and they stood together under the shade of the green and yellow striped umbrella enjoying the cool, sweet break from the heat. Manny licked at his cone with the neatness of a cat, being careful not to stain his suit with the sticky drops of lemon custard flowing down his hand. By the time they had finished, Manny seemed to have shed his stormy mood, and they continued on their way.

They made many more stops that day. Although Eddie didn't ask questions, his disappointment at being left outside must have been apparent in his expression. At one point Manny shot him a look.

"What? I let you tag along, didn't I? How do you think I can do business with a damned kid like you hanging on to my coattails every minute?" Then, his expression softening just a little, he added, "Look, I have to drop something off at Sol's Pawn Shop, near my next stop."

Taking a small notebook and pencil out of his pocket and jotting something down, he tore the slip out and handed it to Eddie along with a small package wrapped in brown paper.

"Can you take this to Mr. Wolf while I'm making my last call?" he asked.

"Sure. Right away," Eddie grinned shyly, glad finally to have a chance to prove that he could be useful.

Sol's Pawn Shop was a hole-in-the-wall located on 9th Avenue between two bail bond businesses. Eddie's entrance was announced by the tinkling of bells over the door. A disorderly collection of lamps, appliances, musical instruments, dishes and every other sort of dusty bric-a-brac crammed the tall shelves lining the walls; items too large to fit into shelves covered the floor, leaving little room to walk. Eventually, Eddie located Sol Wolf, a small man with flyaway tufts of wispy gray hair and incongruously black eyebrows that looked like woolly bear caterpillars. Sol sat hunched over a battered wooden desk behind a dusty counter. Crammed in beside it was a fancy mahogany casket with a scratched lid vying with it for space at the back of the store's one narrow room. With one hand, he was maneuvering a messy tuna fish sandwich toward his mouth while the other was busily totaling up the day's receipts. He didn't stop when Eddie came in.

Eddie picked his way through the crowded aisle toward the desk in the back and cleared his throat loudly before saying, "Mr. Silver sent me. He asked me to give you this."

Sol finally stopped figuring and looked up. "Well, well, what does Manny have for me today, I wonder?" Sol said, pushing his chair back and wiping the grease from his hand as he shuffled over. He inspected the note before unwrapping the parcel and spreading the contents out under the lamp on the counter. The package contained a number of small items of jewelry: a pair of earrings with tiny red stones and pearls; a pair of gold cuff links; a watch chain and a silver rosary.

Wolf inspected each item carefully under a small magnifying loupe that he held to his eye and made a notation of its description and value in a tattered green ledger. When he was through, he tucked a receipt and thirty dollars in an envelope, sealed it and handed it to Eddie.

"Mr. Silver's note says you're his associate. So I guess we'll be seeing each other again." He smiled, stuck out a wrinkled hand and shook Eddie's hand.

When Eddie came out, Manny was waiting for him on the corner. Suppressing a smile, Eddie handed him the envelope. He didn't mention that Sol had told him what the note had said.

That afternoon they followed a circular route that brought them back to where they had started. Their pick-ups had taken them several hours, and it was now late afternoon and school was out.

"Time to knock-off for the day," Manny said, and reaching into his pocket, he peeled two dollars off a large roll, folded them and handed them to Eddie, who stood open-mouthed, looking down at the neat green squares resting on his palm.

"Well, you just gonn'a stand there staring like a stunned mullet? I can take it back if you don't want it," Manny said and shrugged, as if annoyed.

"No! I mean yes. Yes I do! Want it, I mean. Thank you, Mr. Silver," Eddie said formally.

Manny started to leave, then turned back.

"By the way, son, you have a name?"

"Uh yeah, it's Eddie. Eddie Boyd," he said, still staring in amazement at his first ill-gotten gains. The fact that he had done almost nothing to earn them didn't dampen his excitement at the feel of money in his hand. He hastily folded the bills and jammed them into his pants pocket. Manny had unknowingly chummed the waters, and Eddie would definitely go back for more.

The following day, Eddie decided to forgo the arcade slots and instead check the sandwich shop to see if Manny might again stop by to see Frank during the lunch hour. If Manny was there, Eddie decided, he might have a chance to go with him on his rounds again. Since Frank had seen him often enough outside the school and in the shop too, Eddie felt bold enough to approach him.

"Has Manny been here yet?" Eddie tried to sound nonchalant.

"What business is it of yours?" Frank asked with a sneer.

"I work for Mr. Silver," Eddie replied, trying to convey an air of confidence he didn't quite feel.

Frank's eyebrows rose quizzically, and he shot back, "Is that so? Well Manny had better watch himself. Certain people might be getting pissed off, and you'd better be careful, too, hanging around him," he warned.

Eddie left without eating, and as he exited he looked up to see Manny crossing the street. Manny had spotted him too, and Eddie tried to stand a little taller.

"You again?" Manny growled.

"I'm here to work, Mr. Silver, like you said," Eddie responded hopefully, thinking of the note.

"I said that? Well, come on," Manny shot back. "I don't have all day to waste standing around talking."

Eddie kept his expression neutral, but he smiled inwardly, and unable to resist a smug glance back at Frank, he fell into step behind Manny.

SEVEN

Before long, Eddie's truancy became a regular thing. Fortunately St. Joseph's was lax in checking absentees, and as long as he was there for his first class, he could usually duck out later. If asked why he didn't respond to roll call in a class, he explained that he had been in study hall and had lost track of time. He tried to make sure, though, to be back at school in time to sneak into Latin, the last period of the day. This class was taught by Father Jerome, who must have been eighty-five if he was a day. His recitations of Tacitus were punctuated with fits of wheezing coughs. He was also blind as a mole. That didn't matter, though, because Father J had taught the same class for so long he knew even the longest passages backwards and forwards. It was his poor eyesight that made it possible for Eddie to make his surreptitious late entrances day after day.

The one downside to his new job was that it meant he didn't have time to see much of Jim. Jim had grilled him about his recent disappearing act. Eddie's elaborate evasions and ruses had failed to convince him. Jim had known him too long and too well to believe excuses like homework or chores. It was clear, too, that Jim was more than a little hurt that Eddie hadn't taken him into his confidence.

But after a while Jim quit asking, leaving Eddie feeling both relieved and guilty. He had forsaken his oldest friend and could find no way to put things right. He couldn't see how he could include Jim in his new life; even if he could, his new association was something Jim would neither approve nor agree to be part of.

On certain days, Manny would say, "Tomorrow I have to see a man about a dog." That meant Manny had other things to attend to, more important jobs than collecting receipts, apparently the kind of business a young assistant should not be privy to. After school on those days, Eddie would fall back on his old pastime and head to his favorite spot, a deserted piece of beach where a rock jetty ran out to deeper water.

It was on one of those days when he had nothing much to do, that he jumped on his bicycle and peddled off toward the bay. The air was damp and heavy. Angry clouds roiled up on the horizon like sooty smoke from an oil fire. When he reached the beach, a buffeting wind was sending waves crashing over the rocks and flinging the salty sea spray into the air and onto the shore. The sand was strewn with an army of dead man of war deposited in and around the seaweed at the high tide line. These jellyfish were not in control of their destiny, but moved at the sole discretion of the prevailing breeze. Their cobalt blue balloon bodies had a frilly ridge along the top. They measured only about six inches in length and looked more like flattened ballerina tutus than sea animals; nevertheless, they trailed long, delicate tendrils that had a deadly effect on small fish and unwary humans alike. In the water, these poisonous filaments trailed sometimes as far as twenty feet behind the bulbous sail. The small partially digested fish they contained attracted many more fish looking for a free meal. Swimming upwards inside the man of war's tendrils, the next fish became one step farther down the food chain as the strands engulfed it and the digestive process continued.

Today the wind had blown hundreds of them ashore. Eddie carefully picked his way among the tendrils that lay in tangled strands of slimy purplish-red along the sand at the high tide line. Even dead, their poison could leave a painful sting. He paused as he walked down the jetty, squatting down to look at a colorful display of sea anemone that made their home in the rocks below the waterline. These flower-like animals were beautiful creatures and came in a variety of vivid colors. They too had tendrils, but theirs were like the delicate petals of a chrysanthemum. He watched them wave in the current. A large trunkfish came near, and the anemones instantly withdrew into their hole without a trace. When it had passed, they slowly bloomed again.

A small damselfish approached one flower and was quickly engulfed by the anemone and immobilized. Meanwhile, a clown fish darted in and out helping himself to portions of the stricken fish, while remaining completely untouched by the anemone's poison. When Eddie was little, he used to wonder how one fish could be immune to the venom that could be so lethal to another. He understood now that the clown fish was providing a useful service to the anemone. To allow the clown fish to clean up the skeletons and scales and other indigestible matter stuck in the jelly was the anemone's way of extending professional courtesy to his garbage man—one hand washing the other.

The wind was stronger near the end of the jetty, and great banks of threatening black clouds were piling up in the west. He pulled his jacket tighter around him. He reached the far point, where he squatted down to retrieve the worn length of wood he had wrapped with fishing line and secured with several extra hooks and his cache of sinkers and bobbers that he kept stashed under a flat ledge of rock. The tide was in, and the wind had whipped up whitecaps on the water's surface. The waves that pounded against the rocks had deposited a thick froth of dirty foam in the crevices.

He pulled his fishing gear from under the rock and was just crawling out to grab a fiddler crab to use as bait when something in the foam caught his eye. It looked like a perfectly good shoe—not an old beaten up piece of garbage that might float up, but a nearly new one. Eddie shinnied down the rocks to where he could reach it. He wrapped his hand around the toe of the shoe and pulled, but it was firmly wedged between two rocks. He pulled again, yanking harder this time. Still, it stubbornly refused to budge. Next time, he gripped it with both hands and put all his strength into it. The shoe suddenly came loose, and Eddie toppled over backward, smashing the back of his head against the rocks.

He had lost hold of the shoe when he fell, and now it rested just inches from his face. Protruding from it was a white, hairy ankle in a checked sock with several inches of shiny, white shinbone extending from it.

"Aw, Jesus!" he shrieked, crossing himself, his voice rising several octaves.

The bone had been neatly sawn; however, much of the flesh still attached to it had been shredded by hungry fish. Two crabs were still attached and fought over a strip of the pale meat. Eddie's hands began to tremble and his mouth suddenly tasted like a dirty penny. He knew he was going to be sick and bent over to throw up. Leaving his fishing tackle where it had fallen, he bolted back up toward the beach, grabbed his bike and peddled home as if banshees were chasing him.

As Eddie ran into the house, slamming the screen door behind him, his startled mother gave him a withering glare. Eddie dashed through the room, hoping the ladies in her bridge club had not noticed the streaks of vomit on his legs and feet or the terrible smell he left in his wake. He locked himself in the bathroom, stripped off his soiled clothing, filled the sink with water and scrubbed himself hard. Even after bathing, the smell of puke and the sight of the severed foot stayed with him.

The only sound at dinner that night was the clinking of silverware against china. The quiet in the room was so intense that the chirping of crickets drifting in through the open windows shattered the silence like the screech of fingernails down a chalkboard. His father didn't seem to notice, but Eddie knew the heavy stillness in the room was just the prelude to the thunderstorm that was brewing behind his mother's eyes. He tried to eat, but managed only a few bites before asking to be excused so he could retreat to the safety of his room.

Before long, came the staccato knock on his door Eddie had been dreading. He knew his abrupt entrance this afternoon wasn't likely to be brushed under the rug. He steeled himself for his punishment.

Like an avenging angel, his mother swooped in and sat down on the edge of his bed, her eyebrows drawn together into a tight knot.

"Eddie, for the love of God what is wrong with you? You're a disgrace! Coming in like a whirling dervish, no shoes, smelling like a sewer, and not so much as a polite nod to my guests! How do you suppose Mrs. Briggs and Mrs. Welborn felt? They must think we live like gypsies. I've tried to teach you manners, but do you listen? No! You think about nothing but playing pirate—and at your age! When do you plan to grow up?"

Without waiting for an answer to her last question, delivered in a hysterical scream followed by a flood of tears, she rushed out of his room slamming the door so hard it rattled on its hinges.

Eddie lay there silent, thinking. Should he tell her about the foot? He was sure she'd probably never let him go fishing again if she knew.

"I won't let it happen again," was all he could manage in the way of a mumbled reply, quite sure she hadn't heard.

*   *   *

Diana stopped the swing with her foot and turned to face him. "My God, Dad, you mean you never told your parents what you found?"

"No," he sighed. "I never told them any more than I had to. It wouldn't have done any good anyway. They would have worried, I'd have been in trouble, and that wouldn't have impressed me much anyway. To me it was all a big adventure. But the real attraction was the money. It was about a year before I met Manny that I'd started noticing the way the 'haves' lived in their big houses with their pools and servants. I was beginning to resent living like a church mouse when it seemed so simple to change that."

Diana shook her head in amazement and resumed rocking.

EIGHT

Prior to those past few months, Eddie hadn't really considered that there was a dark side to mobsters. He had thought of them as members of the upper class like the Flaglers, Crandons, Duponts, and other wealthy locals.

But lying there in bed later that night, still shaken by his discovery at the jetty, Eddie reassessed his former beliefs about the criminal world and all that went with it. He knew his father worked hard, and yet he had never been able to afford to buy a house or even a new car, let alone a Cadillac. Why were others able to live so extravagantly, while hard-working families like the Flannigans, the Mouskouris, the Boyds and others like them just managed to get by?

As he lay in his room that night after his grisly discovery, he remembered one unforgettable day a year earlier when he had seen for himself how the wealthy lived. It was a sunny Saturday morning when his father had driven him in their old Ford across the causeway to a palatial home on Palm Island. When the two massive iron gates at the entrance of the drive had slowly swung open, Eddie had been unable to take his eyes off the scene before him. He had been transfixed, moving like a zombie toward the crowd of other partygoers, never even pausing to look back or shut the car door.

Four men guarded the estate's entrance. They appeared at ease, three casually leaning against the massive, white gateposts and one stationed against the trunk of a nearby palm tree. Guards were not unusual at the mansions on Miami's exclusive islands, but these four were armed, their eyes constantly scanning the cars dropping off guests.

The week before, when he had received the engraved invitation to a birthday party for Sonny, the question of Eddie's attendance had caused a huge family uproar. Included in the envelope was a permission slip his parents would have to sign before he would be allowed to attend. Because Capone had been under the government's close scrutiny for his illegal activity, Mr. Boyd had at first refused to allow him to go. Eddie failed to understand what all the excitement was about.

"What will the neighbors think, a fine young man like you going to a place like that?" he had asked, with attempted but unconvincing conviction.

"What sort of place?" Eddie had asked, feigning ignorance. Mr. Boyd didn't explain.

Eddie's mother had firmly refused to let him attend, but for a different reason.

"Yes, it's out of the question, Eddie. You'd have to take a very expensive present for Sonny. How do you expect us to afford that? You can't give someone like Sonny Capone just any old thing. How would it look?"

"But the invitation says not to bring a gift," he countered.

For most of the morning, the discussion had gone round and round. By lunch, having exhausted every argument he could, Eddie was frustrated and pessimistic. But at the end of the long battle of attrition, he had prevailed. At dinner that night, both his parents had grudgingly agreed to allow him to attend the party. He was sure his victory was the result of his brilliant arguments. In reality, it was simply his dogged persistence that had won out.

By the day the grand affair was to take place, his attendance had apparently become a subject of neighborhood concern. As his father pulled away from their house, he looked straight ahead, refusing to acknowledge Mr. and Mrs. Mouskouri, who stood watching them from their front porch. Mr. Mouskouri had been very outspoken about the whole thing. He had a very low opinion of any immigrant son who would choose a life of crime over the many legal opportunities America had to offer.

The ride to Palm Island seemed to take forever. Finally, without having spoken a word to Eddie during the entire trip, his father had deposited him at the entrance to the Capone estate. Inside, beautiful manicured gardens lush with colorful tropical plants and flowers flanked a wide stretch of lawn. As the guests passed through the front gates, each received a gift: for the boys, a baseball, bat and glove, and for the girls, a large box of chocolates. At the appointed time, Eddie and the other guests, who'd all been milling about gawking at opulence beyond their imagination, were herded toward the spacious grounds behind the house.

A stone path led to a sparkling pool grander than any Eddie had ever seen before. At the far end of the pool, near the sea wall at the back of the grounds, stood a two-story tower. Several men with Tommy guns stood on the guard platform situated below its red tiled roof. From their high perch, they surveyed the grounds and the seawall beyond, paying particular attention to the boats that passed back and forth in the bay.

On the large patio beside the pool, men were arranging tables and chairs under the watchful eye of Mrs. Capone. On one side of the patio, lawn badminton was set up and on the other, croquet. Many guests had already begun to play. Most of them had dressed in their best Sunday outfits and brought swimming suits to change into later. As they dashed back and forth in their gauzy ruffles and starched white finery they looked like a multitude of sweaty angels cavorting at a celestial picnic.

When everything was ready, Sonny directed them onto the patio where several long tables were lined up end-to-end. These were draped with blue and white striped tablecloths and napkins. Place cards had been set at each seat. Eddie and the others filed up and down looking for their assigned spots. When finally they were all seated, Mrs. Capone joined Sonny at the head of the table.

Mae Capone was a smallish woman with brown hair and a plain but pleasant face. Beaming, she welcomed and thanked everyone for coming. Eddie noted that Sonny resembled her in manner, if not appearance. They both had a quiet, almost hesitant way of speaking, as if expecting to be interrupted at any moment. But Sonny's mother obviously adored him, and she smiled down at him as she spoke.

"We have lots of wonderful food—everyone's favorite, fried chicken—and afterward some more games and prizes," she said. "And then, of course, cake and ice cream." Encouraging everyone to eat, she settled at a round table nearby, where she sat fanning herself with a napkin.

Eddie had been so excited thinking about the party he had consumed several glasses of water before leaving home. Before long, his bladder was about to burst. He got up and went over to the table where Mrs. Capone was sitting. He leaned in and whispered in her ear. Giving him a sympathetic nod and smile, she rose and ushered him toward the back entrance to the house.

She was leading him down a hallway just inside when they turned a corner. Wearing only his underwear, Sonny's father hurried angrily down the hall toward them, mopping spaghetti sauce off his chin and shouting. When he saw his wife he screamed, "God damn it, Mae! The maid laid out my brown pants! It's Sonny's birthday party! I told her I wanted the white ones. Where are my white pants?"

Surprised, Eddie pressed himself back against the wall to avoid a collision. With considerable disappointment, he noted that Mr. Capone was pot-bellied, balding, and not much taller than he was. The figure he cut was certainly nothing like the image captured in newspaper photos of the threatening-looking character sneering from under the low brimmed hat.

Mrs. Capone hurriedly turned toward Eddie and pointed at the door to the bathroom then ran down the hall chasing after her husband. Amazed by the scene he had just witnessed, Eddie stood in the hallway for a few moments, listening to Mr. Capone cursing the brown pants, the maid's negligence, and his poor wife. Finally, a door slammed and he remembered what he had come in for.

When Eddie swung the door open, he stood in the doorway holding the knob in his hand, dumbstruck. The room was huge. A floor of shiny, pale-pink tiles sparkled in the dappled sunlight coming through the window. A floor-to-ceiling undersea mural, complete with a triton-wielding Neptune on his throne, decorated three walls. Finally gathering his senses and letting go of the cool knob under his fist, Eddie positioned himself before a conch-pink toilet with a seat of genuine mother of pearl. He was so impressed by its magnificence he almost hated to pee in it.

By the time Eddie got back outside and joined the others at the table, the waiters had begun serving platters of fried chicken, corn on the cob, baked beans, and baked apples. Pitchers of lemonade and baskets of biscuits were being passed around. He wondered how anyone could possibly be expected to have room for cake after such a feast.

While the guests greedily attacked the food, a man dressed in full cowboy regalia performed rope tricks on a small portable stage set up near one end of the pool. At one point, the cowboy's assistant released a small fox terrier from a cage. At a cue from the cowboy, the dog darted over, and leaping in and out of the spinning lariat, he began jumping rope. For the finale, the cowboy stepped up on the diving board and held out a flaming hoop. The little dog hopped up onto the board and dove right through the fire and into the pool.

As the cowboy was collecting his equipment and his assistant was toweling off the wet dog, the backdoor opened and Sonny's father stepped out. Now fully dressed in a white suit and grinning widely, he walked over to the cowboy and pounded his back like they were old friends. While they were talking, a uniformed waiter wheeled out a three-layer birthday cake on a teacart. He rolled it over to the head of the table where Sonny was sitting and lit the candles while an accordionist began playing Happy Birthday.

On the ride home after the party, Eddie had sat with his eyes closed replaying in his mind everything he'd seen that day.

"How was the party?" asked his father.

"Oh, it was okay." Eddie sighed. He couldn't see the good of trying to explain what he was feeling, knowing that it would probably just result in another lecture about the sin of excess.

*   *   *

As he lay there on his bed, now a year older and a year wiser than he was then, Eddie stared up at the crack in the ceiling above his head.

He could still recall every detail of that beautiful mother-of-pearl toilet seat and the feel of its lustrous, smooth surface. He mused with just a touch of shame that if people like Sonny's family could be accused of the sin of excess, he was surely just as guilty of the sin of covetousness. He wondered what sort of penalty he would incur if he traded the one sin for the other.

*   *   *

NINE

The newspaper smacked the screen door each morning at six-thirty sharp with the regularity of a rooster's crow. Ed was usually up before the sound broke the stillness and had already put the coffee on to brew. He would retrieve the paper, fix himself a cup, and on most days by the time Diana came out of her room, he had already finished reading everything that interested him. But today was Sunday. Diana got up early every Sunday and insisted on preparing a big breakfast for the two of them before they left for church. She dressed the table in a white linen cloth and bustled about, hurrying to get the food ready by seven-thirty sharp. If everything went as planned, they made it right on time for the nine o'clock mass at St. Josephs.

Ed sat and watched her serve up the eggs, French toast, jam, bacon, orange juice and coffee. She insisted on using the best china. He remembered the one time he'd tried to persuade her to use paper napkins and plates. She'd rolled her eyes in exasperation.

"When was the last time you used the nice dishes, Dad? Are you saving the good stuff for your wake, or what?" she had needled him. "Really," she went on, "do you always have to be such an ascetic? It's not a sin to enjoy life once a while."

He smiled now, thinking about it. No, he hadn't always been so. There had been a time when he'd had very little interest in abstinence of any kind. But he remembered too how life often pulled the rug out from under you with no warning at all.

*   *   *

On Wednesday mornings, students attended early mass, during which they prayed the rosary for the souls of all the faithfully departed, may they rest in peace. Amen. The sharp edge of the kneeling rail ground into Eddie's kneecaps making it impossible for him to concentrate on anything but pain. Father Horka's voice droned through an endless string of Hail Marys. Eddie usually got half way through one Hail Mary attentively before he found himself counting the dust motes floating through the shaft of sunlight streaming through a cracked stained glass window in the choir loft. Now the pain brought him back to reality, and he fervently prayed for the last prayer to be over soon.

The first period of the day was English, and his class had been reading Dante's *Divine Comedy*. The topic of that day's discussion was Dante's placement of souls in Hell, Purgatory or Heaven. Father Horka lectured in a dramatic and ominous voice:

"Within the Inferno," he said, "Dante places not only sinners but also illustrious pagans such as Homer, Ovid and Horace. In the section we'll cover today, these damned souls, naked and pale, wait to be taken across the river to the Underworld by Charon, the boatman." He began reading,

> 'And lo! Toward us came, upon a bark,
> An ancient man whose hair was long and white.
> He cried: 'Beware, beware, ye guilty souls!
> Nor ever hope to see the sky again:
> I come to take you to the other bank,
> To everlasting gloom and flames and ice.'

Father Horka paused here to emphasize that even the virtuous pagans were damned to hell because they had lived before the birth of Jesus Christ. As usual, Eddie began drifting off after a few minutes. Suddenly, Father Horka's voice stabbed him in the ear like an ice pick.

"Eddie? Eddie? Eddie, if it wouldn't be too much of an intrusion, would you please read from Canto Four of the Inferno?"

Eddie knocked his book off his desk so he could find Canto Four without giving away the fact that he'd been asleep. He flipped pages until he found the place and began to read the words of Virgil, Dante's guide through the inferno:

'My goodly master said:

You do not ask me who these spirits are

We see about us. Ere we pass beyond,

I wish to tell you that they have not sinned.

Though they are worthy, this does not suffice,

Because they never have received the joy

Of holy baptism, essence of your faith.

But those who lived before the time of Christ,

Could never worthily adore their God:

And I myself am of this company.

For this defect, and for no other wrong,

Our souls are lost: for this we must endure

A hopeless life of unfulfilled desire.'

Eddie stopped reading and looked up. "But that's not fair, Father. It wasn't their fault they were born before Christ. It's God's fault. Why should they be in Hell for something God did," Eddie argued, "when the lustful, the bad popes, and the harlots all get to go to Purgatory, even though they sinned by their own choice?"

"Ah, but after death even Virgil accepts his fate," said Father Horka. "Isn't this true, Eddie? It is one of the great mysteries of our faith. Whether one's sins are willful and intentional or simply the result of ignorance or weakness, it is our acknowledgement of guilt and acceptance of responsibility for a wrong done that eventually cleanses the soul and helps us find peace."

Catholics were lucky, he explained, even those who sinned purposefully, because through confession they were granted the chance to get into Heaven after spending a certain amount of time doing penance in Purgatory. This privilege was theirs just by virtue of their faith in Jesus.

Eddie didn't understand this mystery of faith thing at all. If God didn't want humans to understand him, why did he give them rational minds, the gift that placed them above the animals, as Father Horka liked to say? Eddie added this to the list of other things he had begun to question. Things like un-baptized dead babies being doomed to spend eternity in Limbo and the whole question of indulgences. What kind of sin could a newborn baby have on his soul? How could money buy forgiveness from God? Eddie was sure even thinking about these questions was probably a sin. Where was the logic behind the mysteries of God's mind? He started to ask Father about this, but decided not to risk it.

His last morning class was history. Lunch followed that, and as usual Eddie sneaked out the back door and wandered over to the shoeshine stand hoping to spot Manny. He leaned against the wall eating his sandwich trying to look like he was waiting for a friend. Manny was in his usual spot, sprawled in Junior's chair thumbing through a racing form and eating an apple.

Junior was a permanent fixture in this arcade and had been polishing shoes at this stand as long as Eddie could remember. Unlike some older Negro men whose shoulders had a deferential slump and whose heads drooped forward, Junior carried himself with great dignity. He was at least seventy years old with a crinkle of silvery hair and a gold incisor. He always wore a black vest buttoned all the way up and a crisply starched white shirt with gartered sleeves. He was missing the little finger on his right hand. Eddie had asked him about that once. Junior told him how he had been born a slave on a plantation in Mississippi and wasn't freed until he was five. He had lost the finger, he explained, as a punishment for stealing an apple from his master's fruit bowl.

Junior was just getting started, and Eddie sat down on the step to watch him work. In those days, shining shoes was an art form, and Junior was a consummate performer. His materials, various colors of paste wax, an array of brushes, polishing cloths, and liquid lampblack for outlining the soles, were kept in a divided tray to the right of the footrest. He began by spitting on the rag before dipping it into brown polish. Leaning intently over Manny's left foot, he worked the wax into the dark leather. Then the show began. Pulling a clean flannel rag from his back pocket, he grasped it at either end and began buffing. He worked his cloth like an instrument, and with the panache of a percussionist, his hands beat out a snappy, syncopated rhythm. In his gartered white shirtsleeves, he reminded Eddie of a New Orleans jazz musician he had once seen on a Mardi Gras poster. Junior buffed until the leather of both shoes shone like polished bronze. Finally satisfied, he twirled the cloth in the air, stuffed it back into his pocket, and grinned at his masterpiece. The shine went for fifteen cents, and Junior's show was worth every penny.

Manny folded his racing form, slipped Junior his usual dollar and started toward the Arcade's exit. He seemed to notice Eddie for the first time, and glancing back over his shoulder at him said, "You coming?"

That afternoon, they walked west from the arcade's back entrance on First Avenue and Second Street and continued on toward Flagler Street, downtown's main thoroughfare. At its east end, Biscayne Bay sparkled like an aquamarine gem between the crowns of coconut palms and Poinciana trees that lined the water's edge. Across the street, hotels, fancy shops and theaters were set behind a majestic row of royal palms lining the west side of Biscayne Boulevard. The farther one headed west down Flagler toward the courthouse, the older and seedier the commercial establishments became, as the wide, welcoming building entrances nearer the bay were replaced by plainer, narrower doorways advertising bail bonds, loans, and cheap walk-up rooms.

Even after the lunch hour, downtown's main street was still crowded with office workers on the late lunch shift. A block from the arcade, Eddie and Manny passed the consulting office of Dr. Seward, Phrenologist. Eddie paused to look at his window display. Prominently featured was life-sized white porcelain bust with the naked head divided into twenty or thirty sections all outlined in black. Neat calligraphy in each region explained its function and relation to various ailments that could be discovered by examining the bumps on the head. Dr. Seward was reading the head of a fat man seated in his leather examination chair. Eddie would normally have stopped to watch, but Manny seemed in a hurry.

When they came to the fruit stand at Second Avenue, Manny stopped to exchange a few words with Sammy Siegel, the owner. Sammy sold tropical fruit, coconuts, carved coconut husk masks, conch shells and cheap trinkets to tourists from the North who wanted vacation mementos to share with family members and neighbors back home. When he saw Manny, Sammy stepped from the stall's shady interior, wiping his hands on his apron.

"Who's your handsome associate, Manny?" he asked.

Reaching into a crate of oranges wrapped in green tissue paper, Sammy selected two, peeled them and handed one to each of them. Sammy and Manny walked toward the far corner of the stand speaking in low voices to each other. Eddie couldn't make out much of their conversation, but suddenly Sammy smiled, displaying a mouthful of long, crooked teeth and then bellowed with laughter. While they spoke, Eddie wandered through the narrow isles inhaling the luscious smell of ripe pineapple and grapefruit and fingering the long strands of pink and purple shell necklaces. After five or ten minutes, Manny clapped Sam on the back, and motioning for Eddie to follow, continued down the street.

Manny seemed to know everyone in every shop and establishment they passed. As they paused to look at a movie marquee at the Moorish entrance to the Olympia Theater, Manny tipped his hat to the girl behind the ticket window. She smiled broadly, winked and slid two tickets under the window grill. When they got down the block, Manny handed them to Eddie.

Eddie found that whenever he was with Manny, there was always the possibility of an unexpected windfall. They had walked six or eight blocks when they came to a narrow doorway between two old buildings in the lower rent section. A hand painted sign over the entrance promised *Live Girls*.

"Hey, Eddie, you ever been to a peep show?" Manny asked.

Before Eddie had time to reply, Manny had pulled the door open and guided him inside. Eddie, expecting a smoky room with a stage, instead found himself in a narrow brick passage lined on either side with curtained windows. The floor was damp and reeked of a combination of acrid odors and bleach. After the bright glare of sunlight, the sudden darkness inside made it difficult for Eddie's eyes to adjust.

"Come on," Manny said as he guided him forward, one meaty hand on each of his shoulders. At the farthest window on the left, Manny stopped. He punched a black button under the peeling windowsill.

A curtain slid back, and through the smudged glass Eddie could see into a dimly lit space not much larger than a closet. The only two things in the cubical were a rumpled bed and the girl kneeling in its center.

For a moment, he stood with his eyes glued to the floor. Finally, recovering from his embarrassment, he looked up at her. On closer inspection, Eddie could see that this was no girl. She must have been his mother's age if she was a day. He watched in fascination as the woman behind the glass slowly unfastened her robe. She exposed first one shoulder, then the other, and let the top fall open to reveal her breasts. They looked nothing like the milky white, firm breasts of his cousin and her friend when he'd spied on them one night through the crack under the bedroom door. These breasts drooped, and were blotchy and freckled. With a look of boredom, she lay back on the bed and began squeezing them. Then she spread the robe to reveal a puckered belly and a patch of dark hair.

Eddie suddenly remembered Manny. He sneaked a peek at him out of the corner of his eye. Manny wasn't looking at the girl. With a hint of a smile, he was watching Eddie. Eddie's face grew hot with a blush that spread right up to his eyebrows. Somehow the whole thing had lost its appeal. Even if she'd been pretty, Eddie doubted he could ever enjoy a peep show with someone watching him.

"Hey Mr. Silver, it's getting late," he mumbled. "I gotta get home before my mother has a hemorrhage. I'll see you later. And thanks for the movie tickets and the . . . uh, show. It was great."

"You bet!" Manny said, slapping him on the back.

Ten

According to the popular song, life is sweeter on the sunny side of the street. Folks up North must have believed it. It was nearly November. If Miami lacked the familiar signs that signaled autumn in the North, it had its own equivalent. Each fall, crowds of Northern tourists descended on the city like drifts of brightly colored leaves. Like a nip of frost in the air, this seasonal increase of business activity pumped the adrenaline of the city up a notch. The yearly tide of visitors had increased with each passing year, keeping pace with easy money, consumerism, and stock speculation.

Like everyone else, Eddie found himself caught up in the heady whirlwind of prosperity that appeared to have no end. Each day offered up new experiences to be tasted and savored, and he was working his way down the banquet table like a starving man.

He had never paid much attention to financial news. His ears usually perked up only when the subject was gangsters, movie stars, or fishing. But he wasn't blind and deaf. Of course he had heard the recent talk about the stock market. At school, Father Horka said that the boom had eventually to slow to a realistic and more consistent pace, and that the recent dips in the stock market were to be expected as part of the process. These latest downturns just signaled that the unbridled joy ride, as he put it, which everyone had been enjoying, was slowing down a little.

The previous week Eddie had listened with more interest as his father read a newspaper article reporting that the market had taken a sudden dive, bigger than anyone could remember. Now that was all anyone could talk about. He began to notice a hint of panic in the hushed voices of the men gathered together in small knots in the arcade discussing the daily reports from Wall Street.

On Friday when Eddie met Manny, he asked him what he thought. He knew he could depend on Manny for an honest answer, and one he could understand.

"Well, I wouldn't worry about it, Eddie. You haven't been buying on a margin, have you?" Manny smiled the way he did when he was pulling Eddie's leg.

"What's that?" Eddie asked curiously.

"That's when you buy stock and only put a little down and pay the rest on credit," Manny explained. "If the stocks go up, then you're in the chips. You sell some off for a profit to pay the broker. You have the rest earning you a nice little bundle. But if they go down and you've put your house or car up as collateral, then you might find yourself hoofing it and sleeping under a bush. You don't want to get in hock to the bank, Eddie. Brokers and bankers are just bookies in suits. As long as they're making their money, everybody's happy. But you better not miss a payment. You know what I mean?"

This explanation helped Eddie better understand the degree of rising panic he had recently begun to see in the faces of the men in the arcade. That night at dinner, he tuned in more than usual to his parents' conversation. His father insisted that there was nothing to worry about. Since he wasn't invested in the market, they were safe, he said. Eddie breathed a bit easier. His mother quickly dispelled all the relief he had felt.

"Millie Sherman told me today that her husband's company is already losing investors, and they're cutting back on production and laying off employees. Charlie lost his job. They don't know how they're going to make expenses," his mother sighed, lighting another cigarette. She took a long drag, blowing the smoke out through her nose like Marlene Dietrich in Blue Angel. This new habit of hers really irritated Eddie. He rolled his eyes when she wasn't looking. The gesture looked mannish. Besides, he hated the way she always grabbed on to every passing fad.

"Well, the newspapers aren't going to fold, are they? People still need the news, and the newspaper needs photographers," argued his father.

"Yes, I suppose you're right," she sighed, shrugging her shoulders. Eddie noticed that as usual she refused to acknowledge that her husband's menial job was keeping food in their mouths.

In the harsh glare of the dining room lamp, his parents' faces looked as impassive as chiseled stone. He wasn't sure whether they were just trying to reassure him or whether they really believed they would remain untouched by the fickle scythe of the economic reaper. Eddie clutched their hopeful words to his heart with a small but welcome measure of relief and went to bed glad for once that they weren't rich. At least they didn't have anything much to lose.

A week later, the conversations at school circled around the economy with the persistence of a flock of hungry buzzards. Most students knew next to nothing about the causes or possible results of the current situation, but a lack of knowledge rarely stopped them from engaging in heated debates about any subject. Arguments raged back and forth between the older students as to the seriousness of the matter.

Some said it was just a lot of hooey, just something cooked up by the government to keep everybody riled up. Others, like Eddie's mother's friends, had begun to experience the first shock waves of the declining market. The nervous questions and high-pitched voices of some students echoed the tension in their families as they spoke of lost jobs and fear for the future. Bob Curran's uncle, whom everyone knew was richer than Midas, had reportedly lost everything he had in less than a week. A few others, Eddie among them, sat silently and a little embarrassed by their own good fortune. During the heated discussion, Sonny, too, squirmed in his seat and said nothing.

Father Horka always seemed to know when his students needed to bring their worries out in the open, and he put down the textbook he was holding and let them talk. In a tone more subdued than usual, he tried to explain the crisis and the possibilities they were facing.

"In the past few years, class, the wealthy in this country have been in control," he said soberly. "They've driven the prices of some stocks so high that now they're worth more than the assets of those companies. We've been living fast and loose, buying everything on credit, wanting to have it now and pay for it tomorrow." His voice climbed a notch higher. "And on top of that, we've been bankrolling half the world. Take Germany, for example. We have been supporting the Germans and half of Europe since the end of the war. And now if we don't watch out, this Mr. Hitler and his band of thugs will be making more trouble, and we'll be back there before we know it putting out new fires!" Suddenly he was shouting, his flushed face bright red. He stopped and walked to the window trying to collect himself. Then he cleared his throat and began again more softly. "I'm afraid we are all going to have to make some sacrifices before this is over."

Outside the classroom window, sunlight glinted off the shiny chrome headlamp of the Cadillac parked at the curb in the No. Parking Zone. The sharp glare reflected back in Eddie's eyes, and momentarily blinded by it, he shielded his face with his hand. The room had grown silent; some students sat shuffling their feet in embarrassment and others looked at their hands or fiddled with their shirt buttons. Shaken by Father Horka's uncharacteristic display of emotion, they were just beginning to absorb the fact that the future, which they had always seen as bright and sure, was perhaps less certain than they'd thought.

*   *   *

ELEVEN

Diana had spent the day at the hospital sitting with her friend Marion, who was recovering from a hip replacement. The wind was gusting hard, driving sheets of stinging rain in its path, when she dashed in through the kitchen door shortly after seven to find the house dark.

"Dad? Dad?" she called, shaking the water from her umbrella and propping it in the stand in the corner.

Hearing no response, she hurried anxiously from room to room. She had reached the living room before she finally heard him call to her.

"I'm out here on the porch," he yelled. "The wind is really kicking up. I just came out to enjoy the show."

"Well, come on in now. It's getting late and it's too windy and wet for you to be sitting out here."

She went back inside, switched on the TV and turned the volume up so she could listen to the local news while she made dinner, and Ed would be able to hear, too, since he was a little deaf. Usually she had to repeat every other word to him—aside from the commercials, which were obviously intended for the hearing impaired. Once she had him settled in his easy chair, she returned to the kitchen to make bell pepper and meatloaf sandwiches with leftovers from last night's supper.

The weather was the major story at the top of the hour. All the local stations were following the progress of the latest hurricane currently located just southeast of Cuba and moving northwest toward the Florida Keys.

"You think it'll hit here?" She stuck her head out of the kitchen and shouted over the blaring pizza snack commercial.

"Looks like it might," he shouted back, "but this one is small. And anyway, this house is brick and built to take it. No trees in the yard to blow down either."

"No trees, no shade either," she said under her breath, "but I guess that's one advantage."

"This one might blow some water in around the windows, but it's nothing like the '26 hurricane. That one was worse than Hurricane Andrew. They quit building frame houses here after that one. They found out then you'd be safer in an up-turned umbrella than one of those things. I was about twelve then. Now that was a hurricane!"

*　　　*　　　*

The first warning signs that a great storm was brewing began late one afternoon. Banks of dark clouds were gathering in the eastern sky. The sun was shining, but fierce gusts had begun to whip the tops of the tall coconut palms in the yard with increasing frequency.

That day Eddie, Jim and Peter Mouskouri had been lazing around outside. When the wind's relentless buffeting collapsed the lawn chairs and sent them tumbling toward the thick hedge of oleander bushes in the corner of the backyard, they ran to secure them then beat a hasty retreat to the safety of Peter's house. Thunderstorms were common in Miami, and Eddie loved to watch them. He ran to the window and looked out.

The wind continued to increase over the next few hours and grew so violent it occasionally bent the uppermost trunks of the palm trees nearly horizontal to the ground. Each new onslaught sent loose fronds and coconuts crashing down. A few minutes before seven o'clock, George and Sophia rushed in from the market.

"You boys go home quick," George said urgently. "Bad storm is coming, big hurricane. My brothers hear other fishermen talking. This one is very dangerous," he warned.

Hearing the fear in his voice, Jim and Eddie rushed for home. As Eddie dashed across their adjoining yards toward his front porch, he turned to stare at a large wooden barrel that was clattering crazily down the street in front of his house. He had to bend over into the wind just to keep from being blown over. Now tree limbs, awnings, boards—anything that had not been tied down—sailed through the air like bits of street trash in the wake of a dust devil.

He finally reached the porch and scrambled up the steps. Just as he clutched the doorknob, the wind ripped the door from his grasp, nearly tearing it from its hinges. It crashed into the room leaving a knob-sized hole in the plaster. His parents had been standing at the front windows anxiously watching for him, and as he entered, his mother rushed over to help him push the door closed.

"This is some storm," his father exclaimed, staring out at the rapidly darkening sky, which now glowed with an unnatural green light shot through with racing brown-tinged clouds.

"You're not scared, are you?" Eddie asked him.

"Well, I've never seen anything as bad as this," said his father with a concerned frown.

Beatrice, who was terrified of storms, grabbed her rosary beads, shut herself in the pantry and refused to come out.

Within an hour the winds had surpassed gale force, and they continued to increase steadily all during the night. When a great gust brought down a major power line, their home and all those in the neighborhood were plunged into complete darkness. Eddie's mother felt her way to the kitchen and came out with a lantern that she carried with her as she hurried about lighting candles in every room.

The storm blast shook the window casements, each new assault bowing the thin glass. As the panes shifted in their wooden frames they produced an eerie high-pitched creak, a sign they were close to splintering. Every time this happened, Eddie cringed, certain that the next strong gust would shatter them and propel a hail of razor-sharp shards hurling toward his face.

The wind wailed, and the driving rain began to seep around the edges of the window frames and spill onto the floor. A growing lake of water now flooded the southwest side of the house. Anne frantically mopped while Eddie wrung out the rags and towels into two tin buckets.

Suddenly, something huge crashed against the roof shaking the whole house. Eddie and his mother dropped their rags and rushed toward the source of the sound. When they reached the dining room, they stopped and stared in shock. A jagged hole in the ceiling revealed a patch of angry sky. In the gray-green shaft of light filtering in from above, bits of broken roof tiles, lath and plaster swirled down into the room like confetti. Each violent gust of wind brought with it a curtain of water that soaked the already flooded carpet. The huge branch that had fallen through the roof rested on the dining room table.

Eddie ran to his bedroom window. Through the waves of blowing rain, he could see that the huge Poinciana tree in the front yard had been completely felled by the storm. A second upper branch was wedged into the roof at the front corner of the house. As it had fallen, most of the tree's roots had been ripped out of the ground and now reached skyward like a many-fingered hand.

The storm raged on all night. At first light, Eddie peered out the window and watched in wonder as several large sections of someone's roof sailed by. A driverless car rolled down the street, pushed before the wind like a toy.

Just after dawn, almost miraculously, the wind and rain suddenly stopped. The sky became lighter, and anxious to see what the storm had done, Eddie cautiously ventured into the front yard. The streets were completely flooded, and those yards not underwater were littered with debris. Telephone poles all through the neighborhood were either leaning precariously or had fallen down altogether, their dangling power lines sparking and crackling where they touched the ground. Electricity was fairly new to their neighborhood, and until then, Eddie had not fully realized the danger posed by exposed wires.

A mongrel dog that lived on the next block stumbled, unaware, onto one of these. In horror, Eddie looked on, as it first grew stiff then began jerking and dancing in the shower of sparks. The poor animal's fur smoked, and the air stank of burning hair. Eddie was about to act on his impulse to run to help him when his father, watching from the window, burst out the front door and shouted.

"No, Eddie! Don't touch him! You'll be electrocuted!"

The house across the street had lost half of its roof, and the carport had collapsed, crushing their Model T beneath the rubble. Jagged shards of glass lay everywhere, along with heaps of wood, awnings, tree limbs and twisted lawn chairs. At another house down the block, the windows had blown in. Just inside, in the midst of the debris, Eddie could see their neighbor, Mrs. White, sitting in a chair sobbing while her husband gently dabbed at the blood trickling down her forehead and cheek and tried to soothe her.

Then, just as suddenly as it had stopped, the winds began again with renewed fury, this time from the northeast. Having thought it was over, Eddie was caught by surprise and had to make a dash for the house.

When it was finally over, some homes, Jim's and Eddie's among them, had sustained some damage but survived. Others were not so lucky. In the aftermath of the storm, Eddie and Jim had wandered around stunned by what they saw. Three blocks in from the waterfront, two forty-foot fishing trawlers had been destroyed and washed ashore by the storm surge and now rested incongruously in the middle of the street.

Eddie had returned home that day to find his father slumped over the kitchen table wiping tears from his face with the back of his shirt sleeve. Eddie had only once seen his father cry. That was on a happy occasion when he had drunk too much at his niece's wedding and begun reminiscing about how quickly time passed. This was different. A sober man crying meant something serious, a major catastrophe, had occurred.

"Is it Mom?" Eddie asked fearfully.

When his father failed to answer, Eddie saw then that the hole in the roof had destroyed more than a few pieces of furniture. His father was holding several pasteboard boxes of glass negatives he had kept stored next to the table linens in the dining room closet. Thinking to protect the delicate images from becoming scratched, he had carefully sandwiched paper prints between each glass plate. The water from the storm had dissolved the albumin emulsion on the paper, sticking everything together and ruining both prints and negatives.

Destroyed along with the fragile images of Rudolph Valentino and Pola Negri, Cornelius Vanderbilt and all the others, was the entire record of the best work of his career. Photographs of people and events he had captured at a single instant in time had been wiped out just as quickly.

The 1926 hurricane was the first major disaster of Eddie's life. Like most of his friends, his initial excitement at the awesome power of the storm itself had overshadowed his understanding of the seriousness of its aftermath. Eddie and Jim, at first overjoyed to remain home for the month it took to repair the school, soon learned that for many in the community, much more than their homes had been devastated by the storm's fury. For them, the following months would be a difficult time of slow and painful recovery.

Eddie's family was among those whose lives would be forever changed after the storm. In addition to the destroyed negatives, his father had also lost most of his equipment. The storm flood had ruined several of his best cameras. As the water-soaked leather bellows dried, they split at the folds, and corrosion ruined the delicate shutter mechanisms. This loss struck the final blow to his hopes of returning to a career as an independent photographer and thus had forced him to seek a full-time position at the *Miami Herald*.

Eddie's attendance at St. Joseph's was the one sign of social status his mother stubbornly refused to relinquish. She swore that if necessary they would eat beans at every meal before she would allow him to attend a public school with the common riff-raff.

The storm's ferocity had a profound effect, too, on the most ambitious and treasured of Eddie and Jim's plans as well. It had now become obvious to them that they would never reach Tahiti in the loosely formed boat of their imagination. With this certain knowledge, their naïve optimism crumbled under a new, more cautious view of reality and an unexpected phase of manhood began.

*   *   *

"That was when I first learned," Ed said to Diana, "just how much one event could overturn everything. The few luxuries we'd enjoyed before the storm disappeared afterward, in order for my parents to keep me at St. Joseph's. We did eat a lot of beans and we walked a lot, too, when we couldn't afford to put gasoline in the car."

"What an amazing story!" Diana marveled, as they sat at the table listening to the wind rattle the screen door. "I've never even heard about that hurricane. I hope this one doesn't hit," she added, "even though this house is brick and we don't have any trees to fall through the roof. Now I understand why you never planted any, but I'd still like to have one for some shade on the porch," she laughed.

By the next morning, the hurricane had been downgraded to a tropical storm. When Diana returned to the hospital to check on Marion, the wind had decreased but rain was still falling.

Ed sat on the porch and watched the decreasing downpour. Funny, he thought, that no one today seemed to worry much about hurricanes and recessions and wars. He wondered why. He'd have to remember to ask Diana about that. As the swing gently rocked, he reflected on how profoundly that one natural disaster had affected everyone for years afterward.

Even when the storm was just a memory, his youthful optimism had remained considerably dampened. Before the storm, such emotional outbursts as Father Horka's might not have impressed him. Afterward, he began to fear that other events in life could be as unpredictable as the weather. Like a bolt of lightening, tragedy could strike at any time, and every day it had been harder for him to remember, much less escape, into the safe world of childish fantasy.

*   *   *

TWELVE

Eddie had fallen into a regular routine of showing up for school in the mornings and, when he could find the opportunity, working for Manny a couple of afternoons a week. Sometimes he ran errands or made deliveries, and other times he just tagged along to see what might turn up. As the economy in the rest of the country continued to get worse, the activity that kept the underworld busy was still going strong. During the season, Miami still drew crowds that came for the sun, horse racing and available liquor.

"Hey, Manny," Eddie asked him one day, "you got any kids?" Manny's expression was guarded, and he didn't seem to hear.

"I'll bet you a nickel you do," Eddie said.

"Do what?"

"Have kids."

"Now what would I do with a kid? I don't even have a wife."

"Well, don't you get lonesome?"

"With a pest like you around?" Manny smiled and put a big arm around Eddie's shoulder and knuckled him on the head. Eddie laughed then and smacked Manny's big arm.

Eddie had begun to feel completely comfortable around this gruff man he knew operated outside the law. He did learn, however, that there were certain things he should not talk about. He found that out pretty quickly. When he crossed the line into these forbidden waters, Manny's scowl was a clear storm warning.

One Saturday when Eddie was hanging around Dinner Key, he noticed a larger than usual crowd milling about Pan American's barge, which served the newly created airline as both ticket office and passenger lounge. As he crossed the dock leading out to the structure, Eddie looked around, expecting to see a seaplane about to land or one about to take off. Either of these events often drew crowds eager to watch the show. This day, he couldn't spot anything in the air, and only the usual moored boats lay in the water beyond the barge.

Twenty to thirty people had gathered at one corner of the barge, and those in the front were leaning over the railing looking down at something in the water. Eddie elbowed his way closer to the edge of the crowd of onlookers and impatiently craned his neck to peer over the shoulder of the man in front of him. What he saw made his breath catch in his throat. Floating face down in the water, a bloated form bobbed up and down on the surface of a large oil slick. The body was wearing a white shirt, gray pants, an alligator belt and one alligator shoe. The distended form looked somehow incongruous surrounded by the beautiful oily halo that spread around it like a wide rainbow on the surface of the water. Two men had rowed out to retrieve it. One reached out with a gaff, snagged it by the collar, and pulled it alongside the boat. They turned it over. The swollen skin of the drowned man had lost all color and looked artificial, like the wax pears in his mother's fruit bowl. Eddie didn't want to see any more, but he couldn't tear his eyes away. The right side of the head was gone, and the left eyeball dangled from the socket. Several fiddler crabs were fighting over what was left of the tasty morsel.

That afternoon Eddie told Manny what he'd seen.

"Do you think they'll find out who he was?" he ventured. "He must have been in the water for a long time and it was hard to tell with half his face gone."

Manny frowned.

"Probably just some drunk that fell off the pier," was all he said, but something in his expression, a brief flicker behind his eyes, told Eddie to drop the subject. This was one of those things better left alone.

Most of the time now, though, Eddie looked forward to his trips with Manny. He had begun taking more interest in his appearance, making sure his shirts were pressed and his nails were clean. It had become Manny's custom to slip him a couple of dollars before he left each day, and Eddie smiled with pride as the small stash under his mattress grew.

On a rainy day in early December, they took a new direction, crossing the tracks west of Miami Avenue into the large colored neighborhood. They had never worked that area before. Manny began picking up bags and paying off some of the men. At first Eddie was silent, but his curiosity got the better of him.

"I didn't think we worked this side of town. Has Mr. Capone expanded into the colored section?"

"No," said Manny, "This is mine. I sell a number for just ten cents, but it all adds up. A man has to have a little something of his own going for him."

"Well, what about, you know . . . He wouldn't like that would he?"

"And who's going to tell him? Are you?" Again he examined Eddie with a little more than casual interest.

"Of course not. What do you think, Manny? Jeez!"

THIRTEEN

In school the priests preached that God had invented sex for procreation. They failed to mention that pure joy was an added benefit. They must have known that when the time was right, boys would discover that fact on their own.

The thought had entered Eddie's mind all too frequently lately, but until then he had been satisfied with a hand job, as he and his friends referred to it in their frequent conversations about sex. Eddie's friends all asserted there were girls who would do "it", although most refused to mention any names. One of the guys claimed absolute knowledge. The way to tell which girls were interested was to notice whether they bit off their middle fingernail. Another insisted the girls who sat with their legs crossed and swung their foot were the experienced ones. Norman Crawford knew his sister did it because he caught her at it in her boyfriend's car. He said she was a tease, too, because she sewed collar buttons on the front of her brassiere so when she wore a sweater it would look like she was naked underneath. But they all agreed that even if a girl were a tease, she probably wouldn't really put out, so most of them were still virgins wedded to their own hands.

When they made their weekly confessions, the priest would always prod them with the question, "And how many sins of impurity have you committed?" Eddie had always lied and cut the figure to about half the true number, which nevertheless resulted in a hefty penance of Our Fathers and Hail Marys.

The difficulty of abstinence had been exacerbated further by the fact that the climate of the times regarding sex had become very lax. The new movie industry had led the way, with so much raw sex displayed larger than life on the silver screen that the Pope was eventually compelled to issue an edict forbidding Catholics to view a movie that the Church Decency Board had not personally approved. Eddie laughed, imagining the sour-faced Pope and cardinals sitting around discussing how much breast was too much.

One movie Eddie and his friends saw more than once was *A Roman Scandal*, starring Eddie Cantor. Among other things, it featured twenty gorgeous girls wearing nothing but flowing blond tresses just long enough to hide the entrance to paradise while allowing the puppies' pink noses above to peek through.

Manny casually asked him one day while they were making their collections, "You haven't ever been with a girl, I mean sexually, have you Eddie? I mean, you're still a virgin, right?"

"Me? No! You trying to say I'm some kind of queer, an Ethel? Is that what you think?" Eddie bristled.

"Hey, Manny said, "Don't get in a lather. I was just asking."

Eddie was silent for a time.

"Well, yeah. I guess. I mean, I've got a cousin that's really built, you know, and she let me see hers and I showed her mine."

Manny looked thoughtful. In a bit he said,

"Well, it's time we changed that."

"What do you mean?" Eddie asked.

"You'll see," Manny said.

A few blocks farther along, Manny stopped at old building near the tracks with a sign over the door that read The Greentree Hotel. They entered, and as they climbed the stairs, Eddie couldn't help staring at the paintings of naked ladies that adorned the wall. At the top of the stairs was a large room with upholstered sofas and chairs and a gaudily decorated Christmas tree in the corner. Manny took a seat and motioned to Eddie to join him. When they had settled themselves, six or seven scantily clad women peeked out from the adjoining hallway and waved at Manny.

A buxom, gray haired woman came through the doorway. She seemed to be in charge. She smiled and greeted Manny warmly.

"My friend is here for his first time," he said, winking at her. "I expect him to be treated right," he added, slapping Eddie on the back.

"Certainly, Mr. Silver," she replied, beaming at Eddie and gesturing toward the assembled girls with the practiced ease of a maitre'd.

"Take your choice, honey. Do you like blondes?"

Eddie tried to hide his embarrassment. Was he supposed to pick one? He couldn't think of a single thing to say and sat for a painful minute just looking from one to the other as if trying to make up his mind.

"I know just the right girl for you," she said, gesturing to a red-haired girl in an orange and purple kimono to come over. This one had kept her eyes lowered while the others were curiously inspecting him. She walked slowly toward him, and he saw that she was looking at him now; he shyly met her gaze. She smiled the tiniest of smiles. To Eddie's relief, he thought she seemed a little shy, too.

"My name's Estelle, what's yours?" she asked. She reached out and took his hand and put it on her shoulder. She leaned toward him and he could smell her perfume. "Just leave everything to me," she whispered in his ear.

Eddie was beginning to respond, and he bent over slightly, hoping his arousal wasn't apparent to everyone in the room. Manny, meanwhile, had found a girl to his liking, and the two were talking. Estelle took his hand and led Eddie down the hallway.

Once the door was closed, Eddie faced his second challenge. Exactly how, he wondered, were you supposed to initiate sex with someone you didn't even know? Feigning sudden interest in his surroundings, he paused to look around, grasping a precious moment in which to collect his wits.

The room's scant furnishings included only what was necessary for this one activity. It was a small space that contained a bed, a small bedside table that held an ashtray and lamp with a purple tasseled shade, a single chair, a coat rack and a marbled topped washstand; that was the extent of it. A lacy white curtain covered the room's one window. On the wall by the bed was a large ornately framed mirror, but besides that, there was not a single picture or personal object anywhere. He thought the only thing in the room that Estelle might have chosen herself was the lampshade. It didn't take long for him to complete his tour of the ten by ten space.

When he turned back to her, Estelle had slipped off her kimono and hung it on the coat rack. She now stood before him, seemingly as comfortable as he was nervous. She regarded Eddie with an expression both innocent and wise, and Eddie thought of the eyes of a great sea turtle. She sat down on the bed and held out her hand to him.

Eddie lay down next to her and she snuggled up beside him. In the soft light coming through the thin curtains, the pale skin on her shoulders with its light scattering of freckles looked too fragile to touch.

She made encouraging small talk as she slowly unbuttoned his shirt. While she helped him out of it, he struggled to shuck his pants off by wriggling his legs together. He only managed to get them firmly stuck around his ankles. Smiling, she bent down, removed his shoes and then slowly pulled his pants off.

"Next time, take your shoes off first," she suggested, giggling.

Eddie blushed, mutely berating himself with a string of self-deprecating expletives that would have made a sailor proud. All this activity had severely deflated his pride, but in her expert hands it was quickly restored. She showed Eddie what to do in a slow and patient way.

He was a quick learner, and before he knew it his curiosity was satisfied and his virginity happily left behind. When he was through, he expected her to jump right up like she was on the clock. But instead she put her arm around him and sighed contentedly, as if she had really liked it.

"You did that like you had lots of experience," she lied sweetly.

Eddie flushed scarlet, an idiotic smile spreading across his face.

"I hope you'll come see me again, Eddie," she said and kissed his cheek.

When Estelle led him back down the hallway, he jumped at the sight of a uniformed policeman sitting on the sofa in the lobby talking quietly with the older woman he'd met earlier. He shrank back against the wall. Fearing it might be a raid, he asked Estelle what they should do.

"Come here, you poor little bunny," she said, and pointed out the window. She giggled. "See that armored car down there? That belongs to the chief of police. He's collecting his percentage. That car will stop at every house in town today."

Manny and Eddie left The Greentree and made their way east on First Street. Eddie was thinking about Estelle. When he joked that he might have to earn more money to cover his new diversion, Manny snorted but said nothing.

Eddie had noticed something back at the hotel. No matter the color of the hair on their head, most of the girls except Estelle had black pubic hair. When he mentioned this, Manny roared with laughter.

"You really are green, aren't you? Women can bleach or dye the hair on their head any color they want, but if they mess with the other they can get a bad burn. That can put them out of business for a day or two. When the hair on their crotch matches the hair on their head, that's their natural color."

Eddie felt stupid not to have thought of that.

When they were almost back at the school, Manny stopped.

"Wait here," he said, and disappeared into a shop.

In a moment, he came back out carrying a large parcel wrapped in cellophane.

"Merry Christmas, Eddie. You and your family have a nice holiday."

He thrust a huge basket of assorted fruit, nuts and candies into Eddie's hands. Then he peeled off a ten-dollar bill and tucked in into his shirt pocket.

"You're getting expensive," he said. "I guess I'll have to find you a better paying job."

Eddie walked home whistling, thinking how he could come up with a believable explanation for the fruit basket. He wondered whether tomorrow would be too soon to stop by The Greentree to see Estelle again.

FOURTEEN

Father Horka kept a quote by Oliver Wendell Holmes hanging in a fancy frame above his desk. It said, "A man's mind, once stretched by a new idea, never regains its original dimensions." It suddenly dawned upon Eddie what Holmes had been thinking about when he wrote those words.

Christmas had come and gone, and for the first time Eddie hardly noticed. When he had forgotten to come home to help decorate the tree on Christmas Eve, his mother insisted on checking to see if he had a fever, sure he was coming down with something. The new red tackle box with Eddie's name on it under the tree Christmas morning elicited only a cursory glance from him, and he returned the new cribbage board to its wrappings without even looking at it.

When Eddie had first entered into his partnership with Manny, he had been worried that his mother might notice his newly acquired income and grill him about its source. He had prepared several stories to explain where the money had come from, none of them very plausible. He needn't have worried. He had underestimated the number of visits to Estelle he would soon be making. He had no problem spending all his profits. He even worried he might be forced to go to a loan shark.

"Bless me, Father, for I have sinned," Eddie began. "It has been three weeks since my last confession, and these are my sins. I took the Lord's name in vain six times." He paused to think of some other venial sin to confess. "I lied to my mother about my grade in history."

"Yes, go on," Father Horka urged. He yawned.

"I went to a prostitute," Eddie mumbled. Father Horka's beads clattered to the floor on the other side of the thin wall that separated them. His robes rustled as he shifted position to retrieve them. He leaned his head closer to the screen as if he thought he might have misheard.

"You went where?"

Eddie cleared his throat. Father was making him repeat himself. This was the oldest trick of the confessional.

"Uh . . . to a . . . prostitute?" Eddie's voice came out in a raspy whisper.

"How many times?" he said a little louder. Eddie now obviously had his full attention. He tried to remember if anyone he knew had been sitting in the pews close to the confessional. He hoped they couldn't hear.

"Eight," he whispered.

"What?" Father's voice shot up another decibel.

"Eight." Eddie could hear Father's heel tapping against the wooden seat rail.

"That must be pretty expensive. Where did you get the funds?" Father said.

Eddie knew he was in for it now. "The money?" He cleared his throat.

"The money. Yes! The money! Did you steal the money?"

"No, Father, you think I'd steal? I won it playing the slots," Eddie lied.

His already black list of sins was growing like a cancer right there in the confessional.

"You've been gambling?" Father's breathing became faster and his voice got louder.

"Well, yeah, I was gonna confess that," Eddie hurriedly added. "You know, just nickels."

"Gambling and seeing a prostitute. I see. These are serious sins. Very serious. These are sins that will land you in hell if you don't watch yourself. Do you want that?" Father enunciated each word with staccato-clipped clarity.

Eddie had begun to sweat. Father didn't know the half of it. This was going to require a big penance.

"I want you to say fifty Hail Marys and make a good Act of Contrition," he said. With a sigh of relief, Eddie began to rise when he added, "And be at church every Tuesday night this month for the Stations of the Cross."

Eddie left the confessional feeling more guilty and miserable than when he'd walked in. He didn't want to go through this again, but how could he go to communion without going to confession?

As he left the church, Eddie caught sight of his reflection in a cracked pane of glass in the heavy oak door. The fractured image that leered back at him looked grotesquely distorted and more than a little evil. Although Eddie still didn't understand God's mysteries, for the first time he felt thankful that in His omniscience, God had created a purgatory for the lustful and the harlots.

The next day was New Year's Eve, and Manny was uncharacteristically silent all day. As he and Eddie finished their rounds, Manny suddenly turned to him and asked, "Are you pretty strong, son?"

"Sure. I can handle guys twice my size. I'm skinny, but I'm tough enough," Eddie assured him.

"Well here's the deal," said Manny. "There's a boat coming in tonight, the cases are heavy, and you'd have to be quiet and fast if you're going to work for me. Can you handle it?"

"Sure." Eddie tried to keep the excitement out of his voice. He couldn't help remembering the first time he'd seen Manny at the water's edge issuing orders to the men unloading the banana crates. This might turn out to be his one chance to do something more than penny-ante stuff, and he didn't want to blow it by sounding like a stupid kid.

"OK," Manny said. "I'll pick you up at six-thirty tonight on the corner of S. W. Eighth Street and Miami Avenue. Dress in dark clothes. Be on time. I can't be waiting around for you."

Later, Eddie gulped down his supper and changed into navy school pants and a sweater. They were too hot for the warm night, but were the only dark clothing he could find. He knew his mother would give him a tongue lashing if he ruined his good clothes, but he could clean or replace them with the money he would make.

He decided he might need Beatrice's help. Beatrice had diapered him and walked the floor with him and couldn't deny him anything. At times like these, Eddie felt guilty taking advantage of her, but he knew even if she had doubts about his comings and goings, she always kept his secrets.

"If my parents should ask about me tonight, Beatrice, "tell them I went to a movie," he said on his way out the door.

She looked at him with concern, a mixture of emotions flickering across her usually placid face. "You be careful, Eddie, and don't be too late," she finally said, watching him hurry down the walk.

The night felt heavy as Eddie walked toward the agreed meeting place. The humidity clung to his face and neck like a damp veil. The sweater was hot. He looked up to find the stars but couldn't see any.

When he got to the corner, a milk truck sat idling at the curb. Manny sat in the driver's seat, and he motioned Eddie in beside him. He was a little late, but Manny didn't comment. Eddie wondered how he had managed to acquire the vehicle. The cargo bay was vacant and dark, emptied of its usual towers of bottle racks.

"Are we picking up anyone else?" Eddie asked.

"This is a special load. It's just the two of us," said Manny. "We gotta make a run to Palm Beach. If you do a good job, I'll cut you in, and you'll be able to see your girlfriend at The Greentree as often as you like."

The breeze that blew through the open windows was fragrant with the sweet smell of jasmine but did little to cool things off. Eddie was perspiring profusely. He fidgeted nervously, a hundred questions racing through his mind. Would this delivery come in where the other one had? There must be many unmarked channels known only to bootleggers. He wanted to talk, which was what he usually did when he got antsy. But Manny was quiet, and Eddie took his cue from him. He wanted to prove his mettle on this job and was determined to show Manny he could be silent when the situation required it.

They drove down an unfamiliar road to an overgrown area a hundred yards or so from the water, where Manny skillfully navigated the truck through the weeds and low sea grape bushes. After they had snaked through the underbrush for fifteen or twenty yards, Eddie could make out a clear set of tracks running straight to the water's edge, where a boat sat waiting. The man operating the boat stood silhouetted in the dim light. It was Alderman, the runner who'd made the delivery the first time Eddie had seen Manny.

When Manny saw who it was, his back stiffened, and an odd expression flickered briefly across his face, but he said nothing. Manny climbed out and told Eddie to wait in the truck until he called for him. This time, paying no regard to his shoes, Manny waded out to the boat and helped Alderman drag it up a few yards closer to shore. They exchanged a few brief words but mostly were quiet and businesslike.

The cases were heavy, and sweat continued to pour down Eddie's face. They worked quickly and silently stacking boxes into the cargo bay. Eddie lifted and pushed without a word. Lightened of its cargo, the boat rose higher in the water. As the load was transferred, however, the weight in the truck increased, and the back tires sank deeper into the sandy ground. Just as they were throwing a tarp over the crates, a harsh crunch of tires on gravel broke the stillness, drowning out the quiet lapping of the water. Manny jerked his head in the direction of the sound. Another van was approaching from the same direction they had just come. Its headlights were out.

"Let's get out of here!" The urgent note in Manny's voice sent Eddie running, and he bolted into the passenger seat.

Manny jumped behind the wheel of the milk truck and gunned the engine. For a moment the wheels spun uselessly in the soft sand. Manny pushed the gear lever into reverse, allowing the tires to rock backwards, and then threw it back into first gear. Two repetitions of that maneuver finally bought some traction, and they sped off.

In a few dozen yards, there was a turn-off Eddie hadn't noticed on their approach. Manny swerved onto it and took off down a different rutted path than the one they had come in on. Their load was heavy, and they hit the deep potholes in the road with such force that Eddie's head slammed into the roof sending sparks flashing across his eyes. Nearly losing control, they skidded several times, careening over the high mound of packed sand between the two deep ruts in the road. Though oppressive, the humidity brought them a bit of luck. It kept their dust to a minimum, preventing the telltale cloud trail that would show up in headlamp beams, making them easy to track. Manny's eyes were riveted on the tracks ahead, and his white knuckles gripped the steering wheel. Finally, the dirt track intersected with a narrow paved road that led them out onto Biscayne Boulevard.

Eddie's skin prickled with the adrenaline rushing through his body. For that brief moment they'd been stuck in the sand, Eddie caught snatches of conversation between Alderman and two of the men in the other van. They had seemed more confused than accusatory. When they had jumped out and questioned Alderman, they hadn't roughed him up or handcuffed him. So they weren't the police as Eddie had first thought. He couldn't keep silent any longer.

"Who were those other guys?" he asked Manny.

"I'd hoped to be out of there before they arrived," was all he said. He was still driving very fast, constantly checking the rearview mirror. Eddie turned in his seat and stuck his head out the window. Several cars were following far behind them, but none looked like the other mysterious van. Without warning, Manny made a hard left at Thirteenth Street and pulled into a driveway behind the Pig and Whistle Barbeque Stand. They sat and waited for what seemed like a long time. Manny's breath whistled through his smashed nose in time with Eddie's racing heart. Finally, he seemed convinced he had lost whomever had been following them, and they pulled out and continued north toward Palm Beach.

Eddie had learned when to be quiet, and the rest of the trip continued in silence. Finally, they arrived at their destination and pulled into a neighborhood of large, expensive houses. They stopped briefly before a two-story residence at the end of a cul-de-sac, then turned into the long drive and followed it around toward an open garage in the back.

Eddie could see the lights of a huge Christmas tree shimmering in the big bay window at the side of the house. Faint peals of laughter and the sound of a tinkling piano came from somewhere inside.

They began unloading the cases and stacking them in the garage. Their frantic getaway and the growing realization of what they had just done had left Eddie feeling fearful and emotionally exhausted. As he worked, his muscles quivered from the earlier exertion, and the load now seemed much heavier.

When they were through transferring the boxes, Manny knocked on a door at the back of the garage. A tall man in a tuxedo answered and ushered him inside. Eddie climbed back into the truck, shut his door, and fell back against the seat, glad the night's work was over. He must have dozed off. Manny came back and slid into the driver's seat, shocking Eddie awake. Manny handed him two crisp twenty-dollar bills without comment.

The drive home was uneventful, but Manny's usual casual smirk had turned into a dark scowl, and he reeked of sour perspiration. Pulling to a stop at the curb where he had picked Eddie up, Manny leaned over the seat and put a hand on his shoulder.

"Listen, Eddie," he said. "Tonight could have been dangerous. We'd better stay out of sight for a couple of weeks. You still have some time off school for the holidays. I'll find you after things cool down."

The milk truck slid away from the curb, and Eddie paused to watch it disappear around the corner. He slowly turned and began the long walk home. By the time he reached his street, most of the houses were dark. The clouds that had covered the sky earlier had dissipated, exposing a full moon. A bright, hazy ring around it signaled a coming storm.

As he neared his home, Eddie sidestepped piles of gaudy icicles, cardboard fireplaces and discarded trees that had been set out for the trash man. In the moonlight, their straggling wisps of tinsel shimmered, a last, small reminder of their earlier splendor. They looked sad, like lonely old ladies with smudged mascara, garish rouge and hard lips waiting at the corner for the last bus. Most years, he would have rescued one of the smaller trees to put in his back yard and adorn with bits of fruit and nuts for the birds. But this night, he just didn't feel in the mood.

FIFTEEN

Although Eddie continued to be Estelle's best customer during the week, he also began to see her on Sunday, her day off. Because the girls weren't supposed to fraternize with the customers, they'd arranged a meeting place where they weren't likely to be seen together. They'd usually take the jitney to Miami Beach, where there was a nice, nearly deserted spot between 78th and 79th Streets. Estelle would bring a blanket and a picnic lunch, and Eddie would bring a book and his fishing gear. They'd spread a blanket on the sand, eat their lunch, and Estelle would sunbathe while he read or fished in the surf.

Eddie had begun to discover that Estelle was quite intelligent and wise beyond her years. She was also quite pretty. She had the peaches and cream complexion of a natural redhead, mischievous gray-green eyes and a smile that brought dimples to her cheeks when she laughed. When they went out, she wore no makeup and in her beach clothes looked even younger than her eighteen years. Though Eddie was shy and quiet around the girls at school, he felt totally comfortable with Estelle.

She loved to be read to, and on their outings to the beach, he would indulge her with a chapter from whatever book he was currently reading. Fitzgerald was Eddie's favorite writer. Although Hemingway's rough heroes and distant locales appealed to his thirst for adventure, it was Fitzgerald's writing that held the greatest appeal. His descriptive passages played out in Eddie's mind with the clarity of a motion picture. He especially loved Jay Gatsby. He was a character Eddie could really understand. Eddie dreamed of the same universe of ineffable gaudiness that young James Gatz longed for, and like him, Eddie yearned to reinvent himself, to experience an exciting life totally unlike the mundane existence he had been born into.

One day after Eddie had finished reading to Estelle, he decided to chance asking her about something he'd been mulling over but had been afraid to bring up. He hated the thought of offending her and possibly jeopardizing their relationship. Just then, he was lying on his back with his forearm thrown across his eyes shading them from the glare of the sun. Eddie plucked up his courage and grabbed the moment. In the event his question made her angry, he wouldn't be able to see her expression. After mentally rehearsing and then rejecting several lead-ins to his query as too tactless, he decided on an open-ended approach. She could respond with as little information as she liked, but he hoped she might open up and tell him more than he had asked.

He cleared his throat and began in an off-hand tone of voice,

"How long have you been at The Greentree?"

She was silent for so long he lowered his arm and turned to look at her. Had he committed an unpardonable blunder?

She was gazing out into the water with her back to him. "It seems like forever, but it's only been a year and a half," she responded softly. She didn't speak again for a long moment. A bad sign, Eddie thought. Finally, she lay back beside him, turning her face toward his.

"My mother died when I was ten. My father remarried again four years later, and his new wife just didn't want me around. I thought it would be better for all of us if I left. So one day I just took off. I got on the bus in Tallahassee and headed for Miami. When I got here I was doing okay for a while too, working at McCrory's Five and Dime. But it wasn't very long before, times being what they are, they had to let me go. Then, it was take what I could find, or be out on the street. I was lucky to have a friend who got me on at The Greentree after she went to work there. It's really not so bad. I mean, at least I don't go hungry." She looked searchingly at Eddie. "And I got to meet a nice guy like you, didn't I?"

Relief flooded over him. From that moment, in Eddie's eyes at least, Estelle became as pure as Dante's Beatrice. She was just someone down on her luck like so many others; she had only done what she had to do to survive. And still she seemed to be able to approach life without resentment of her past or her present circumstances. She was practical and optimistic, and when Eddie was with her, he found he could forget his present dissatisfaction with life and simply enjoy the moment.

"How did you meet Manny?" she asked, changing the subject.

He explained how it had all come about, and she listened with interest.

"I think you've been good for him," she said when he had finished.

"What do you mean?" Eddie's eyebrows shot up.

"At The Greentree, he's like family. All the girls know he took it hard when his wife left and took the kids."

"What? What wife and kids? He told me he wasn't married."

"Well, she's been gone for a while. She didn't like his business associates, said he was setting a bad example for his children. One night, he came home to an empty house. All she left him was a letter saying she'd taken the kids and gone away. She told him not to bother looking for them, that she was taking them as far away from him as she could. His family meant everything to him. He tried to find them, but she covered her tracks pretty well. He was so sad for a few weeks I thought he might go crazy. Then, a few months ago, he seemed to snap out of it. That must have been when he met you."

Eddie turned over and shut his eyes so she couldn't see the confusion and hesitation in them.

Sixteen

Most of January passed without any word from Manny. Eddie had spotted him several times at the arcade near their usual meeting place, but Manny didn't approach him. His look warned that the time wasn't yet right, so Eddie spent much of his free time that month hanging around the Pan American barge. He never tired of seeing the seaplanes take off and land and dreamed of someday flying in one.

Each day's newspaper announced a new aviation record. Only a few short years ago, Lindberg had made his first trans-Atlantic flight. For a while, everyone was even singing a popular song about it. Then Amelia Earhart—a woman, of all things—was setting records of her own. Things that had seemed impossible one day were becoming a reality the next.

Lindbergh had carried mail with him on several of his flights, and the prior year the U.S. Post Office had decided to initiate regular airmail service. Key West had been chosen as a base for overseas flights.

A fellow named Juan Trippe was a regular visitor to Miami. As an ex-naval pilot, he had returned from the war and attempted to establish a charter service for wealthy New England socialites, but that had failed. Now he had approached some of his society friends and government officials to invest in a new overseas airline. It was reported that he was making Miami his base, and the city had welcomed him with open arms.

Trippe spent much of his time on the dock overseeing operations. He became a familiar figure to everyone who spent much time around the bay front. It was a warm day when Eddie spotted him and two other men in suits standing on the end of the barge opposite the terminal area looking out over the bay. Eddie followed their gaze from where he stood on the dock, and in the distance, he could just make out the glint of an aircraft dropping down out of the clouds. As it neared, he was able to see the familiar shape and pontoons of the Sikorsky S-38, referred to with affectionate disparagement as "The Duck" because of its odd shape. As the pontoons touched the water, they sent a shower of spray into the air, momentarily creating a rainbow of mist. In a few minutes, it was motoring toward one of the empty berths. When it was secured to its mooring, the door of the little eight-seat craft opened and the pilot climbed out. He climbed down the ladder, turned and offered his hand to help his companion, an attractive woman wearing a pale green dress with a matching cloche hat, descend to the dock. The pilot dressed in a navy blue suit and wearing a leather flight helmet was a good head taller than Trippe and the other men around him. To an aviation buff like Eddie, he was easily recognizable.

Trippe and the other two men welcomed Colonel and Mrs. Lindbergh with handshakes. After a brief conversation, Lindbergh escorted his wife to the terminal shed and then returned to converse with the other three.

The four men stood around admiring the plane. Lindbergh slapped the nose of the little craft and stroked the skin of the fuselage like a jockey caressing a winning racehorse. He was excitedly explaining to Trippe and the others the improvements he had planned to make to the design of cockpit. The more he spoke, the more animated he became, gesturing with his long arms and pacing back and forth. He looked very young in person, so young that Eddie was surprised at the ease with which he wore his fame.

Eddie had nothing else to do, so he spent the next hour or two watching the activity around the dock. He was still there when Lindbergh and the two men in suits boarded the craft again and took off. He watched the stubby little plane ascend into the low clouds, execute a banking turn, and head southward. Just as Eddie was about to leave, he again heard the purr of an engine in the distance. Soon, the plane was back in sight, and Eddie's heart raced to see it set back down on the water with the ease and grace of a gull.

When later that evening at dinner, Eddie said, "Guess who was at the barge today?" his mother raised her eyebrows.

"Who?"

"Lucky Lindy," said Eddie, smugly anticipating their amazed reaction.

Oddly, his father showed no surprise at all.

"The government is initiating airmail service to South America and the Caribbean and they've asked Lindbergh to design their routes," he said. "That's why he's here. The paper is sending me out to the dock for photos tomorrow afternoon."

Eddie's mind raced. He would give anything to go along with his father on this assignment. Finally, he took a chance. What could he lose by trying?

"That would be something to get to meet him," he ventured, trying to lead his father toward a decision but hoping he sounded off-hand, like a grown-up.

"Well, I guess you could come along and help me with my gear."

"Okay!" Eddie shot back before his father could change his mind or his mother could squelch the idea.

SEVENTEEN

All the next day, Eddie was a mass of nerves. He tapped his pencil, chewed off the eraser, fidgeted with the change in his pocket, impatient for the day's classes to end. He could barely stay in his seat. His gaze was glued to the window, and Father Horka finally paused as he passed Eddie's desk to ask whether anything was wrong.

"No, I'm fine, Father," Eddie assured him.

"Well, I'm not convinced," he grumbled. "You look like a person with something on his mind. You'd better concentrate on this assignment, or pray very hard tonight if you expect to pass the test next Monday."

"Yes, Father."

All afternoon, the hands of the big clock in the front of the classroom seemed stuck. Time stood still, and Eddie felt like a fly trapped in honey. When the final dismissal bell sounded, Eddie raced for home. He found his father waiting for him, packing the last of his loaded film clips into a leather case that he handed to Eddie.

"Let's get this stuff in the car," he said impatiently, as he hurried out the door. "We're supposed to be at the dock at four."

They parked by the barge and hurried toward the terminal shelter. Following close behind his father, Eddie straightened his shoulders and tried to look like a photographer's assistant. His father pushed the screen door to the terminal office open, and Eddie, right on his heels, let it slam shut behind him with a loud bang drawing a sharp glare of disapproval.

Lindbergh and Trippe were leaning over a table inspecting a large map on which red and blue lines radiated out from Key West to various points south. The loud entrance caused them to look up.

"Ah, the photographers. We're ready for you," said Trippe. "Lead the way, gentlemen." He gestured toward the door.

Eddie watched Lindbergh's every move. He didn't act the least bit shy; on the contrary, he seemed totally at ease before the camera, casually posing as his father tripped the shutter and captured image after image: Lindbergh and Trippe smiling, a helmeted Lindbergh leaning against the fuselage of the Sikorsky, his scarf fluttering in the breeze, Lindbergh and Trippe shaking hands and holding a sheaf of letters.

The session went smoothly. When the light was nearly gone outside, his father decided to get a couple of exposures of the two men inside with the map. These would require the use of flash powder. Finally, Eddie's assistance would be required. He beamed.

With his father's help, Eddie got the flash tray ready, measuring out an exact amount of powder and sprinkling the mixture along the length of a wooden tray perched atop a telescoping pole. Producing a flash was a delicate process. Too much power would produce too much light; too little, not enough. With preparations completed, Eddie took his position and held the tray while his father opened the camera shutter. When he gave the signal, Eddie lit the powder. It took several shots to insure a correct exposure.

When they were finished, they began to pack up the equipment. Eddie had followed his father's instructions, maintaining his silence throughout the entire operation; now he exploded with a flurry of questions for Lindbergh, determined not to allow the opportunity to speak to him slip by.

"How is it up there? I mean when you're flying," Eddie asked. "Don't you get sleepy? Do you ever worry that your engine will fail? What do you do if you have to pee?"

"Oh after a while it just feels natural," he smiled. "Just like driving a car, only without the traffic. And no cops either. But if you tend to get seasick, it's better not to eat before flying. It can get a little bumpy up there if you hit any weather, and the cockpit is a pretty small space, if you know what I mean."

Eddie stuck to Lindbergh's heel like a piece of gum. He was so captivated he was oblivious to his father's subtle hints that it was time to leave. Finally, thrusting the camera case into Eddie's hand, his father hooked his finger through his belt loop and pulled him out the door with an apologetic wave.

EIGHTEEN

Eddie's father announced at dinner several nights later that he had been given another photo assignment for the following week. This one would involve a trip and sparked much more excitement in him than the last job had. *The Herald* was planning an article on the growing arts community in Key West, and Edward was being sent to take photographs of Ernest Hemingway in his new home there. From Key West, he would fly on to Havana. Lindbergh and Tripp were scheduled to stop there on their return flight from Panama for discussions with Governor Machado about a Cuban base for the new air service to South America.

"How would you like to come?" he asked Eddie between bites of poached flounder, spoken as casually as, "Pass the butter." He went on, "Your mother is convinced you're becoming a barbarian. She insists it would improve your manners if you were to come along. I told her no, but since you've shown me you are learning to handle yourself, I've reconsidered."

Eddie couldn't believe his ears.

"Since I'll be busy pretty much all day," his father continued, "you'd have to amuse yourself. You might want to explore a bit while I'm working. And you'll have a chance to ride the train. The overseas railroad is an impressive piece of engineering. Then we'll fly down to Havana. You're interested in airplanes, so what about it? Would you like to come?"

Eddie opened his mouth then shut it. He glanced at his mother and paused to swallow before he spoke, trying to keep from sounding overly enthusiastic. He didn't want to give either parent ammunition to reconsider.

"Well, I guess so," he said. "How long would we be gone?"

"Oh, just for a few days. We'd have to leave early Friday morning, though, because it's an all day trip to Key West."

With so much to think about, Eddie hardly slept that night as he imagined the trip in great detail. A trip would also involve some other planning. Even though Manny was still keeping to himself, Eddie would have to find a way to let him know how long he'd be gone. He didn't want Manny to think he just got tired of waiting and stopped coming around.

Eddie hadn't spoken with him since New Year's Eve, and now that nearly a month had passed, he hoped it would be safe to meet. He went to the arcades at lunchtime, and as luck would have it, he immediately spotted Manny at Junior's stand. Eddie circled around, afraid to approach him directly. Finally, Manny looked up and saw him. He smiled but said nothing. He finished his shoeshine but didn't walk over to where Eddie was pretending to window shop. Instead, he nodded slightly in the direction of the cigar shop two doors down.

It was a tiny, narrow place with a long counter behind which shelves stocked with cigars, cigarettes and tobacco hung on a mirrored wall. Toward the back of the shop, a small table and two chairs were wedged into a corner. The proprietor sometimes sat there and read the paper when business was slow. Today, he was waiting on a customer in front. When Eddie entered, Manny was sitting at the table waiting for him.

"Hey, Eddie, how you been?"

"Okay, you?"

"Just keeping my nose clean," Manny smiled.

"Guess what?" Eddie said then, eager to tell him his news. "My father's taking me to Key West and Havana this weekend. He's got to go shoot photographs for the paper. He'll be taking pictures of Ernest Hemingway and Charles Lindbergh."

"Well, now, you wouldn't bull me, would you?" Manny shot back, looking doubtful. "How'd you convince your father to take you along on such an important assignment? Didn't you tell me he doesn't have much time for you and doesn't care much what you do?"

"It's true," Eddie insisted. "He's never taken me anywhere before."

Eddie tried to explain how it had come about, carefully leaving out the part about his parents' growing disapproval of his behavior. He knew divulging that to Manny would be a mistake. After what Estelle had told him about Manny's wife, Eddie didn't want Manny backing off, believing he was contributing to Eddie's delinquency. Nor did he want Manny thinking that he had simply made up the travel story to avoid him.

Manny was silent for a few moments, but he had lost the scowl.

"Well, you're quite the egg, aren't you?" More silence. Manny stared at his hands, lost in his thoughts. He shook his head. "I don't know," he finally said, as if to himself. "You think you'd be able to deliver something for me when you're in Havana?"

"I don't know," Eddie said doubtfully. "I won't know my way around. I could try, I guess."

"There's a guy down there, a supplier you might say, that I'd like to strike a deal with. The U.S. Post Office is slow and risky for that kind of business. The government has the names of these suppliers, especially in Cuba, and they confiscate their mail. He shouldn't be hard to find, though. He manages a cigar shop across from the big park, right in the middle of town by the Presidential Palace."

"I think I could find that."

"Okay," he said. "I'll leave an envelope for you with Junior in an hour. Enjoy Havana, Eddie, but be careful. Hey, and stay away from those prostitutes. You don't want to come back with a case of the clap." He slapped a heavy, familiar hand on Eddie's shoulder and ducked back out into the dark arcade.

For the next hour, Eddie killed time thumbing through magazines while keeping one eye on Junior's stand. When Manny reappeared, Junior was sitting in his empty chair waiting for a customer. He jumped down when Manny approached. After a brief exchange, Manny reached in his pocket as if searching for some loose change then put something into Junior's palm and walked off.

Eddie waited a bit before walking over to where Junior knelt arranging his cans and bottles of polish. The old man looked up, an odd expression flickering across his face. He stood up, and without speaking, dug a sealed envelope out of his pocket. He thrust it into Eddie's hand. Eddie studied it then looked back at Junior. On it, Manny had written *Enrique Diaz*. Eddie tucked it into his pocket and ducked back out onto street. He didn't notice Junior follow him to the doorway, nor did he see the way the old man had stood there gazing after him shaking his head, his brows drawn together in a frown.

NINETEEN

Taking his usual short cut, Eddie slipped through the hedge into the back yard to find Beatrice bent over the black iron pot in which she boiled laundry. She was stirring the scalding clothes with a long wooden paddle. Steam rose from the hot water, and she stopped for a moment to swipe her sleeve across her dripping brow. This was a twice a week ritual—Tuesday and Saturday were the appointed days—and he wondered why she was doing this on Thursday.

"Oh good, you're home," she said. "Would you be so kind as to pull that barrel of rinse water a little closer, Eddie? You and your papa need clean clothes to take on your trip," she explained. "Can't have the photographer and his assistant meeting the likes of Mr. Ernest Hemingway with rings around their collars and dirty cuffs, can we? Your mama would have a fit."

In the years she had been with the Boyds, some of Anne's social pretentiousness had rubbed off on Beatrice. Today Eddie could hear his mother's words, her very inflections, issuing right out of Beatrice's mouth.

Impeccably clean clothes were one of Eddie's mother's extravagances. She was most particular about appearance, and even if the Boyds lacked some of the material luxuries of the very wealthy, Anne Boyd deemed that her family would never wear clothing less snowy white and crisply pressed than theirs.

When he went into the house, he found his mother in his bedroom packing his clothes for the trip. She had gotten out Eddie's very best white linen shirt and long brown pants. He watched from the doorway as she folded them with the same precision she applied to setting her neighborhood teas. The clothes Eddie was to wear on the train were neatly laid out on his trunk at the foot of the bed. Did she think they would be meeting royalty in Key West?

"You remember your manners, Eddie," she warned. "And make sure whenever you take your clothes off to fold them or hang them. You don't want to look like a rag-a-muffin. Remember, people judge you by your appearance."

"Yeah, Okay," Eddie acquiesced. "But I don't think I'll be making a lasting impression on Mr. Hemingway," he added.

"Don't be so sure. We're just as good as the likes of him, and don't you forget it."

She inspected him, spat on her hand and pushed a stray hair back from his forehead then turned back to her packing.

Early the next morning, they began the long drive to Homestead where they would board the train. Mr. Boyd was normally taciturn, so Eddie was surprised when he talked the entire way there.

"They called this railroad Flagler's Folly," he began, uncharacteristic animation crackling in his voice. "Never thought it could be done. It's seven miles between Long Key and Key West, and no one could figure how to string tracks across an ocean of water. But men of vision can do anything, Eddie. All it takes is imagination. Henry Flagler brought in engineers. They said the project could only be accomplished by sinking pilings right down into the coral bedrock on the bottom. Took almost eleven years, but he did it. And when the first train ran, even the skeptics were on board to make the inaugural trip. It's amazing, isn't it Eddie?"

"Uh huh." Eddie had been looking out the window but was tuned in to what his father was saying just barely enough to know when a reply was necessary. Bordering the road on both sides, lush fields of sugarcane swayed like deep green waves stretching all the way to the horizon. A crew of Negro men felled the tall stalks with methodical, circular swipes of their huge machetes while others gathered and piled them high. Seeing this made Eddie wish he had a cane to chew on during the train ride.

By the time they reached Homestead, it was almost ten. At ten-thirty sharp the train pulled out of the station, and they settled back in their seats.

"How far is it from Homestead to Key West?"

"128 miles," his father responded, "and a lot of it over water."

Eddie drank in the landscape that flowed by the open windows. For the first few miles, the train ran overland. Fields of pineapples had now replaced the cane. They lay like a great green and yellow quilt split in two by the dividing tracks. As the sun rose higher in the sky, the metal skin of the compartment began to heat up, very quickly becoming a giant oven. The air coming through the windows offered little relief. Where the tracks ran over land, a fine, white dust blew into the car with the hot wind leaving a dull patina on everything.

Before long, they had left the first of the Keys and were rumbling across a long viaduct that carried them over the span of water to the next Key. There was virtually nothing on either side of them but a fifteen-foot drop to the ocean below. The uninterrupted vista offered no single detail on which Eddie could focus his attention, and seconds seemed to stretch into minutes and minutes into hours. The monotony and heat soon made his eyelids heavy, and he slept on the last and longest viaduct crossing between Long Key and Key West.

He awoke to find his father leaning over gently shaking his shoulder. "We're here, Eddie. Let's go."

Eddie awoke with aching legs, back and neck from the hours of sitting immobile, and his skin was encrusted in a gritty film of dirt and dried sweat. When they disembarked on the dock, he immediately forgot the discomforts of the long, hot train ride.

The setting sun painted a dazzling display of color on the clouds in the western sky, and a cool breeze blew off the ocean.

"We're staying with John Pindar, an acquaintance of mine," said Mr. Boyd. "He has a son just about your age. Tomorrow he can show you around the island."

His father hoisted the big portrait camera and tripod on his shoulder, and Eddie carried their two bags. They walked six or eight blocks along the waterfront and turned down a narrow road called Conch Street. They stopped before a two-story house. It was a sprawling, white frame structure set four feet off the ground on stone pilings. A wooden stairway led up to a long veranda that ran the entire length of the house. The four large windows that flanked the front door on the lower level had neither glass nor screen, but all had shutters that were thrown open to catch the breeze. His father knocked on the door, which was answered by a big, burly man wearing a fishing cap, canvas pants torn off just below the knees and a faded striped shirt.

"Maria! Our visitors are here!" he boomed. "Maria's just about got dinner ready. Hope you're hungry. This must be Eddie." A boy stood behind him. "And this here is Joseph. Joseph, take Eddie and Mr. Boyd up to their rooms."

Joseph escorted them upstairs and showed them where they would sleep. The house was quite large, and they each had their own room. Eddie's room had a big bed hung with mosquito netting, a necessity in Key West where shutters remained open at all times. Unless they needed to be closed against blowing rain, they were kept folded back against the inside wall allowing the ocean breeze to cool the house.

After stowing their bags, they spent the next hour sitting in the Pindar family's comfortable dining room feasting on fried pompano, rice, black beans, and plantains. As they ate, Eddie learned that his father had met John when he had first come to Key West on a fishing trip. John and his family were Key West natives, "conchs", whose families had emigrated generations ago from the Bahamas. They spoke with an accent that was unlike anything Eddie had ever heard. John captained a charter boat and earned his living by taking visitors on deep-sea fishing trips. Joseph said little during dinner, but he seemed at ease and genuinely glad to have visitors. After the meal was finished, Maria cleared away the dishes while the two men retired to the veranda to smoke cigars. Joseph and Eddie were left alone to get to know each other.

"What's it like living in Key West?" Eddie asked.

"It's swell!" said Joseph. "There's still smugglers and pirates here, you know, and all kinds of characters."

He told Eddie about bootlegging, fights and sea chases that made the extreme outpost of Key West sound a lot like the old Wild West. He explained that because they were separated from the U.S. mainland, many Key West residents considered themselves outside the sphere and reach of federal laws, particularly the native Conchs, many of whom were completely lawless.

"They lynched a guy just last week," Joseph said, "for siphoning off all his neighbor's fresh water for his bathtub gin business. That's the kind of thing that can get you killed here," he added.

Fresh water, Eddie learned, was limited to the rainwater collected in the cisterns of every house and establishment. People horded it and used salt water for almost everything except drinking. Although most everyone allocated a small portion of their precious fresh water for the making of bathtub gin for private use, stealing someone's supply of fresh water was a high crime.

"Half the people here are smugglers or bootleggers," Joseph said, "so many that no one takes much notice of it. My father's not," he quickly added, "but he says he charges enough taking rich tourists fishing that it's like stealing."

Mr. Boyd came upstairs.

"I'll be taking photographs all day tomorrow," he said, "so you boys will be on your own. Hope you don't mind showing Eddie around, Joseph."

Eddie had hoped to go along with him and failed to hide his disappointment.

"Don't worry," Joseph said, when Mr. Boyd went back downstairs. "There are lots of interesting things to do here. We'll go exploring! I'll show you where the lynching was. The rope's still hanging right there and the guy's shoe is still on the ground where it fell off when his feet were jerking."

Whether as the effect of the long train ride or the big meal that followed, Eddie soon felt bone tired and said goodnight to Joseph and his family. After killing a few mosquitoes that had managed to sneak into his net when he slid into bed, Eddie fell asleep cradled in the smell of clean sheets and a fresh ocean breeze.

He and Joseph rose the next morning to find both their fathers already gone. They pulled on their bathing suits, ate a big breakfast and started for town. Their first stop was the cannery where big sea turtles captured in nets by turtle fishermen were brought and kept in crawls until they were slaughtered to make soup.

Eddie had always considered these creatures one of nature's marvels. Many times he had watched females hauling themselves up on the beach to lay their eggs. As they traveled from the water's edge up the beach and back, their flippers left marks in the soft sand that resembled the tank treads he'd seen in war photos. This exhausting activity took nearly all their strength. In the water, they were as buoyant and as graceful as mermaids. Once out of the water, moving their great bodies, some weighing over two hundred pounds, took an extraordinary effort. They left the surf and laboriously crawled up beyond the high tide line to excavate a hole deep enough to protect the incubating eggs. The process sometimes took them forty-five minutes or more. In the act of digging, their huge, delicate eyes became filled with sand, and their faces streaked with tears. Finally finished with their exhausting labor, they would crawl back into the sea. Eddie never watched this ritual without experiencing a profound sense of wonder at the determination of these great creatures.

Putting them in these concrete enclosures was the cruelest thing Eddie had ever seen. He ached to set them all free. Minding his manners, he said little as Joseph explained the importance of the export of turtle soup to Key West's economy. Eddie didn't care, though. He'd rather starve than eat one of the beautiful animals. He breathed a sigh of relief when that part of tour was over.

After leaving the turtle cannery, they passed by the lynching spot, stopping to reverently inspect the forgotten shoe before continuing on to the harbor. There, they leapt off the sea wall and swam out among the huge sailing vessels and fishing trawlers moored just off shore. By holding on to the anchor ropes, they were easily able to haul themselves down to the bottom to collect old bottles, rust-encrusted anchors, spikes and other treasures they brought to the surface for inspection.

Two or three six-foot barracudas patrolled the harbor like watchdogs. They lay still in the water a dozen yards or so from the boys, watching their every move. As Eddie and Joseph swam from place to place, the huge fish slowly rotated their long, lance-shaped bodies in synchronized motion, as if suspended from a center string. They pivoted 360 degrees, always keeping the boys in their line of sight.

By the time they had finished exploring, Eddie had found an old, coral-encrusted knife and a Spanish coin, and Joseph had brought up a couple of interesting bottles.

For the first time in weeks, Eddie thought about Jim. He couldn't wait to see Jim's face when he got a look at this treasure! With a twinge of guilt, Eddie decided he probably shouldn't tell him, at least not just now.

The rest of the afternoon, they wandered the narrow streets of the city. As the day wore on, the bars began to fill with fishermen who had unloaded their catch and docked their boats for the night. There they sat and drank and traded stories about the day's luck, or lack of it.

Joseph and Eddie went into Sloppy Joe's Bar. Everyone there seemed to know Joseph, and no one minded them hanging around to listen in on the sailors' colorful conversations. Eddie could see why they liked this cool, dim oasis. He looked around, mentally cataloguing everything he saw.

A brilliantly colored macaw paced back and forth on a perch behind the bar. It accepted peanuts from the patrons and occasionally pierced the air with high-pitched screeches. A loud voice boomed from the far end of the bar causing heads to turn. Argumentative, and slightly drunk, a big, red-faced man with a bushy mustache seemed to be holding court. He pounded his fist on the bar spilling drinks and rattling glasses. He was stubbornly arguing with anyone who would listen that blue marlin couldn't be caught with anything but live squid. Eddie recognized him from newspaper photos.

"He's wrong," Eddie whispered to Joseph. "Our neighbors are fishermen and they say that dead bait or big wooden lures are just as good because if you troll with any speed, live bait will die right away anyway."

When they arrived home, both boys were exhausted. Mr. Boyd and Mr. Pindar were sitting again on the veranda. Eddie was curious to find out how his father's photo assignment had gone.

"How was your meeting with Mr. Hemingway? Did you get lots of pictures?"

He frowned and glumly shook his head.

"No. He was already drinking when I got to the house. By noon he was stumbling. I went to load some more film cases, and when I came back he had gone. His wife apologized and said I might find him in a bar down on Duval Street. I took a few more shots of her and their cats, and then packed up my gear. I got enough acceptable photos for the article, but wasn't able to get a good set-up of him in his study. I got what I came for, I suppose," he said, clearly disappointed. Eddie smiled and went inside.

TWENTY

Early the following morning, they set out for the landing strip to meet the pilot who was to fly them to Havana. Mr. Pindar had a charter to take out and couldn't accompany them, but Joseph was itching to see them take off and went along with them to the airstrip. They got to the field to find the pilot already busy inspecting the plane's engines. He stopped to shake their hands.

"Fred Arnold," he introduced himself. "Ever flown before?"

"No sir. This is our first time," Eddie's father replied.

"Here," Arnold said, handing them each a stick of gum. This will help with your ears."

Eddie had no idea how chewing gum had anything to do with his ears, but he took it, thanked him and stuck it into his mouth.

The aircraft they would fly to Havana was a Fokker F-7, built for ground take offs and landings. It was slightly smaller than the Sikorsky that Lindbergh flew. The Sikorsky's high, set back center propeller, thrust-out nose and chopped off tail gave it an ungainly appearance. This aircraft was a lot sleeker and looked more air-worthy to Eddie. It had three propellers, one on the nose and one under each wing.

Arnold started the engines. When he was satisfied that everything looked and sounded the way it should, he motioned for them to climb in.

"How long will we be in the air?" Eddie yelled at him over the loud roar.

"A little less than an hour," he said. "It's only ninety miles. We'll be there before you know it."

Eddie saw Joseph duck beneath the wings and wondered what he was doing. In a second, Joseph reappeared with the wheel chucks in his hands. He held them up above his head, and Arnold waved, turned the plane and eased it forward until it was centered at one end of the long, packed dirt runway. Eddie waved to Joseph who waved back and shouted something, but the roar of the engines drowned out his words.

Arnold pushed the throttles forward, and they picked up speed. The dirt strip had looked smooth from a distance, but as the plane shot forward, the wheels bounced on every stone and tiny rough spot in their path. As they continued to accelerate, the vibration of the engines became so violent Eddie's clenched teeth nearly rattled out of their sockets. Expecting the plane to fall apart at any moment, he shut his eyes tight and gripped the seat. Suddenly, as if a puppeteer had pulled a string attached to his stomach, he felt a floating sensation and the bumping stopped. He opened his eyes to find that they were airborne. Arnold executed a graceful, banking turn, and looking down, Eddie could see Joseph running hundreds of feet below and behind, still waving.

Eddie's father was smiling and leaning toward the cockpit shouting something. He hadn't seemed to notice Eddie's white knuckles and stiff posture. That was just as well. If he had, Eddie knew he would have laughed at him for being scared.

No longer quite so terrified now, Eddie took a moment to look around. The interior of the little craft wasn't much larger than the inside of their automobile. Moreover, the walls of the plane's fuselage seemed much flimsier than the sturdy steel body of their Ford. When Eddie looked down at the water below them, his stomach flipped. He tried to swallow his fear along with the sour-tasting bits of breakfast that had risen up in his throat. He imagined the plane plummeting down in a spiraling dive, waves rushing up toward them from below, and the thin wood and canvas-sheathed walls of the fuselage shattering on impact, water filling his nose and throat . . .

"You okay?" his father shouted at him.

"Fine!" Eddie yelled back, a smile frozen on his face.

Finally, getting a grip on his terror, he peered out at the wispy layer of clouds beneath the plane. When they parted he could see the slate-blue surface of the water, which looked as solid as a sidewalk.

"What are those little white spots down there that keep appearing and disappearing?" Eddie asked.

"Those are the white caps on top of the waves," said Arnold. "In a few minutes, we'll drop down to three hundred feet or so in preparation for landing. Then if you look down, you can see sharks, really big ones, right below the surface."

He was right. In about half-an-hour they began to descend through the clouds. The plane bounced and shook. Eddie again gazed out at the wings, which were flexing up and down with each jolt. Why they didn't break off, he couldn't imagine. Sneaking a look at Arnold, who didn't seem the least bit concerned, Eddie tried to concentrate on what lay outside and below them. In the distance, the edge of a shoreline and then a skyline came into view, the buildings glowing white in the morning sun. Just as the pilot had predicted, Eddie could now clearly see a school of hammerheads circling in the brilliant blue of the shallow water. Even from this height some looked huge, at least twelve or fourteen feet, he estimated.

Up ahead, Eddie could just make out the straight, thin line of a landing strip cutting through the green foliage.

"That's Rancho Boyeros up ahead," Arnold said, pointing.

He eased the throttles back and centered the nose between two windsocks marking the end of the runway. The wings dipped first one way and then the other as Arnold made careful adjustments to the ailerons.

Eddie shut his eyes, bracing himself for the crash. Relief washed over him as the little plane touched down, bounced several times, and finally slowed and stopped near a hangar at the end of the field. He breathed a silent prayer and pried his white knuckles from the arms of his seat. Outside, a large crowd of on-lookers waved excitedly.

Arnold shut down the engines and leapt to the ground. A mechanic wheeled a set of steps up to the door, and Mr. Boyd and Eddie climbed down. Then the mechanic turned and led the way to the hangar. A car and driver waited nearby to transport them to the presidential palace where his father was to photograph Trippe and Lindbergh with the governor. A uniformed man held the car door for them, and once they were seated, he loaded the photographic equipment into the rumble seat.

As Eddie took his first footsteps on foreign soil, he absorbed every sight, sound and smell. He was a little disappointed to see that the landscape of the island looked just like that of Miami or Key West. He had somehow thought that each country would look entirely distinct from every other. After all, he had reasoned, lions and elephants lived in Africa, and polar bears could only be found in the arctic, so he figured Cuba would have its own exotic plants and animals.

Several differences, though, revealed themselves as they drove through the narrow streets on the outskirts of the city. This part of the island looked more primitive than even the seediest sections of Miami. Here, many of the buildings were dilapidated, crumbling and leaning. Their dirty stucco was cracked, and large sections had fallen away, exposing the old stone substructure. Clotheslines strung with wash hung from open windows. The drying clothes and the signs advertising *cigarros* and *carniceria* provided the only colorful relief to these ramshackle structures. Men in white pants and shirts, sandals and straw hats lounged in doorways or sat in pairs on benches. Some were as dark as Negroes. They watched with curiosity as the shiny vehicle slowly passed them on the unpaved streets leaving a cloud of dust behind it. Hordes of barefoot children jammed the street in front of the car, some darting back and forth and others running alongside it. Several jumped onto the running board, where they clung to the windows like monkeys, dropping off only when their arms grew too tired to hold on. The driver made no effort to avoid them nor did he slow down. He simply blared the horn and continued on, showing no more concern for them than he would have for a flock of pigeons.

The city's appearance changed as they neared its center, and cobblestone streets, trolleys and motorcars replaced the horses and handcarts of the outskirts. The buildings, too, changed in character. Many were multi-storied and decorated with arches and elaborate scrollwork. The people here were nicely dressed, most of the men wearing white suits and straw boaters. The women wore pretty frocks and sported the latest bobbed hairstyles.

The car slowed when it reached the plaza, a large park with benches and a walkway through the center, surrounded by several magnificent buildings. A sign identified it as the Parque Central. Eddie's heart leapt at his luck. This was better than he could have hoped for. Their driver stopped the car in front of the largest and grandest building and opened the door for them.

"I'll be about two hours," his father told the driver, collecting his equipment.

"Si, Senor. I come back then," he said, and drove away.

"There is a lot to see around the Plaza, Eddie. When you get tired of walking, wait for me over there," he said, pointing to several benches under a large banyan tree across the square.

He hoisted his camera and tripod onto his shoulder and headed off across the street and up the steps of the Presidential palace.

As soon as his father was gone, Eddie began his search. Manny had said the cigar shop was right across from the park. All he had to do was to walk around the square until he came to it. He figured he couldn't miss it. Shops sheltered beneath a pillared portico bordered the central plaza. He passed a café and a newsstand. A large sign in the window advertised Coca Cola. He wished he had the right kind of money. He was beginning to get thirsty. Farther down the row of stores was a barbershop. The entire front of the place was open to the square. Shelves held bottles of blue and green shampoos and hair tonics that glistened in the sun. The barber was shaving a customer reclining in a chair while several sparrows pecked about the floor fighting over wisps of hair. With a full beak, they flew back to their nests high in the tops of the banyan trees. He continued walking.

A few more doors down, a girl leaning against a column smiled at him, a cigarette dangling from her tan hand. She was standing with one hip thrust out, stretching her skirt tight across her belly and under her round buttocks. She was quite pretty with shiny black hair and the whitest teeth he'd ever seen.

Then, he spotted a place that matched Manny's description. The sign said Cigarros e Cigarillos Habanera. The small shop looked very much like the one in the arcade at home, but with all the signs in Spanish. He went in and spent some time pretending he was looking for something specific. A small dark man behind the counter spoke.

"¿Como puedo servirle, senor."

Eddie didn't understand a word of Spanish.

"I'm looking for Mr. Enrique Diaz," he said, hoping the clerk might recognize the name.

"Si, I know him," the man responded in English.

"Where can I find him? I have a letter to deliver."

"He is not here, senor, but he comes after the siesta. Maybe you leave the letter with me? I see he gets it."

Eddie shuffled his feet, looking around and debating his next move. Could he trust him? If this guy thought the envelope contained money, he'd say anything in order to steal it. He had only a short time here, and at least half an hour had passed since his father left.

"What time did you say he'd be in?" Eddie finally said.

"Not until four o'clock, senor."

Eddie didn't want to let Manny down. On the other hand, he didn't want to do something stupid, something that would lead to trouble.

"Well?" said the clerk. "Come on, I make sure Senor Diaz receives the letter. You can trust me, amigo." He smiled, flashing a set of brown-stained teeth.

Eddie hesitated. Finally he reached into his pocket and placed the envelope on the counter. Brown Teeth took it and put it into the cash register. He smiled again.

"Don't worry, my friend, I give it to him."

Eddie left, and as he walked back to the park, he thought about what he had just done. Havana, like all big cities, was a haven for all sorts of characters. To know whom one could trust was a tricky matter. That was for sure. His chest felt tight. He hoped he hadn't made a mistake.

Eddie found a bench in the shade, and for the next hour he sat observing the people and activity going on around him. Here in the richest, most opulent section of city, the contrast between the social classes was impossible to ignore. A well-dressed woman sat nearby bouncing a baby on her knee and watching her older children play. On a bench near hers an old man lay snoring softly. Unwashed and pitifully thin, it was obvious that even in this tropical climate his torn clothing and toeless shoes would provide little protection from the dampness of the night. The woman sang and cooed to the baby, oblivious to the old man's presence, never even looking in his direction. From his seat beneath the same banyan tree, Eddie looked on curiously as the deep green shadows painted her impassive face with the unnatural colors and hard planes of a cubist painting.

Eddie was still watching the people come and go when his father appeared lugging his heavy load down the path. The car had returned and was waiting for them where it had dropped them off. Soon, they were again on the outskirts of the city heading back toward the harbor. His father's smile suggested that his photo session had gone well.

"What did you think of Havana," he asked.

Eddie mentally ran through his catalogue of adjectives. "It was really . . . different," was all he could think of to say.

On the flight home, Eddie was less nervous. He no longer gripped the arms of his seat and now found time to look around. The physics of aerodynamics was a miraculous thing. How something the size and weight of an automobile could remain in the air with only the help of propellers was something he wanted to learn more about. His natural curiosity had returned full-force, and he pondered the knobs and switches on the control panel wondering what each one was for. If he stretched Arnold's patience asking about their various functions, the pilot never let on.

Twenty-one

Several days after the trip, he went to find Manny. He didn't have to look far. As he was leaving the sandwich shop on his way to the arcade, he ran into him.

"Hey, Eddie," Manny said smiling broadly. He had always seemed genuinely glad to see Eddie, and now, it appeared, some of his old sense of ease had returned.

"How was Havana? You remembered what I told you, didn't you? About those prostitutes?"

"Of course, what do you think? Even if I'd wanted to sample the goods, I only had a couple of hours on my own. And I had things to do, remember?"

"You delivered my letter to Diaz?"

"Yeah," he gave an uneasy shrug. Eddie neglected to mention that he hadn't handed it directly to Diaz himself.

"Did he give you an answer for me?" Manny looked hopeful.

"Uh, no, there wasn't time. It took me a while to find the shop, and as soon as I delivered the envelope my father came back for me, and we had to get back to the air field."

That wasn't exactly a lie, but Eddie's eyes squinted a little the way they always did when he wasn't being entirely truthful. Here, he couldn't count on the darkness of the confessional to hide his expression. Feeling transparent out in the broad daylight, he ducked his head when he said it. Manny didn't seem to notice Eddie's ploy and breathed out a deep sigh, as if he had been holding his breath.

"Enrique knows where I am. I'm sure he'll get in touch with me," Manny said. "Good job, Eddie, and I been thinking," he went on, "it's time to resume our collections. We need to make some changes, though. A little caution never hurts, you know?"

In spite of his comment, it was clear to Eddie that Manny was feeling more at ease. He outlined a new strategy, suggesting different meeting spots and new routes to and from each pick up. Eddie suspected Manny's confidence was also bolstered by another fact. Yesterday's newspaper had reported that Capone was currently under investigation for a murder. For the time being, he would probably be too preoccupied with his own troubles to worry about a little money skimming.

They spent a few more minutes talking as Eddie enthusiastically described his adventures in Key West, relating what he had learned about the Conchs' thumbing their noses at Federal laws. When he told Manny about the flight to Havana, he chose to leave out any mention of his white knuckles. Manny looked at his watch.

"I've got to get going, Eddie, he said, but I'm going to Hialeah next Saturday. Wanna come along?"

"Sure!" Eddie grinned at the thought things were finally going to return to normal. After setting a time and place to meet, the two parted, unaware what was about to occur.

On February 15, the news hit like a bombshell. It was all over the papers. On the morning of the fourteenth, nearly all the members of Bugs Moran's Chicago organization, excluding Moran himself, had been ambushed and gunned down in a garage. The shooters, it seemed, had been dressed as cops. "The St. Valentine's Day Massacre," one headline called it, and the moniker immediately stuck. Even news commentator Gabriel Heater led off his radio show with the phrase. The papers pinned the bloodbath on members of the Capone gang, but Capone had denied any involvement. After all, he said, he'd been in Miami. I know I'm good, he was reported to have quipped, but I can't be in two places at once.

Eddie wanted to know what Manny thought, but since he expected to see him on Saturday, he decided he'd wait until then to ask him. Being such big news, Manny would surely bring it up. Eddie busied himself the rest of the week developing the logistics he would need to get out of the house on Saturday without arousing his parents' suspicions.

Manny usually placed his racing bets with one of the numerous bookies he came in contact with, but this Saturday he had decided go to the track. Gallant Fox, who had won the Triple Crown last year, and strong new contender African were racing and he wanted to see them run. Manny always took great pleasure in introducing Eddie to new experiences and decided Eddie should come along.

This would be another excursion into forbidden territory for a kid Eddie's age. Betting on the horses was technically illegal, but the authorities looked the other way because the tracks brought in crowds of tourists and were a great boost to the economy. Knowing his mother would be aghast if she knew he was going to the racetrack, he had invented a story he hoped would sound convincing enough to insure his freedom for most of Saturday.

After breakfast on Friday Eddie approached his mother trying hard to sound casual.

"I promised I'd help Jim and his father paint their kitchen tomorrow," he lied.

"Well, I'm glad you've found something productive to do with your day," his mother replied curtly. The irony of her words made Eddie bite his tongue.

The next morning, after putting on a clean shirt, slacks and suspenders, he pulled on an old, baggy jacket and a pair of his father's work pants over them. He walked casually down the block toward Jim's house and then cut through a yard and backtracked to where he had agreed to meet Manny. He ducked into an alley on the way, where he stepped out of his painting clothes, bundled them up, and stashed them behind a crate of old newspapers to retrieve on his way back home. As he neared the bay front, Eddie spotted Manny's automobile already waiting at the curb. He was standing outside, leaning against the fender reading the newspaper. Eddie grinned and slid into the passenger seat. He waited for Manny to bring up the Valentine's Day bombshell, but instead he spent the entire ride to the track discussing the horses running in that day's lineup.

Hialeah was one of the premier racecourses in the country, and Eddie was excited to see it for himself. They arrived early, which gave Eddie plenty of time to wander through the beautifully manicured grounds and explore the outbuildings. The formal gardens and the ornate fountains executed in carved coral rock had been modeled after gardens of famous Mediterranean villas, and even the Capone gardens paled by comparison.

Manny bought Eddie his own racing form and left, assuring him he'd find him before the start of the first race. Eddie sat down on a low wall surrounding a lily pond and inspected the lineup for each race, planning his imaginary bets. When he had made his selections, he took a break from reading the racing form to watch the crowd.

Hialeah attracted all sorts. There were the over-dressed couples, tourists from the North most likely, who, like Eddie, were impressed by the surroundings. Many of the women wore furs and were wilting in the Miami heat like uprooted hibiscus plants.

He watched a couple coming up the wide path toward him. The fur-clad woman was sweating and furiously fanning herself with her racing form. The husband, dressed more sensibly in a short-sleeved shirt and summer-weight slacks, walked briskly on while she trailed ten paces behind him cursing the heat under her breath. Eddie laughed as they passed him heading toward the paddock. If she was cursing now, he'd like to see her reaction after stepping in a pile of horse shit and ruining her fashionable spectator pumps.

The local regulars were easy to pick out. They lacked the snappy attire of the tourists and were all business. Eddie listened as two men on a nearby bench argued the merits of their favorite picks for the third race.

"Wadda ya mean?" the louder of the two bawled, waving his hand like he was swatting a fly. "There ain't a horse can touch her! I got that straight from my sister who slept with the jockey."

"Yeah?" said the other. "Well I heard she threw a shoe in the warm-up and she's been favoring the left foreleg ever since. You watch her before the race, and see if I'm not right."

Eddie was beginning to wonder where Manny had disappeared to. The first race was about to start, and the crowds had begun moving toward the grandstands. He scanned the sea of people. Over near the paddock, he spotted a hulking figure in a brightly flowered shirt leaning down talking to a jockey clad in bright red and purple silks. Manny saluted the rider and turned to leave. He craned his neck this way and that, also scanning the crowd. Eddie waved his racing form over his head to catch his attention, and grinning, he sprinted toward him.

They joined the spectators lining the rail for the first race.

"We'll watch this first one from here so you can see what a horserace is like up close and personal." He thrust a ten-dollar bill into Eddie's hand. "Here, go place your bet."

"Hey, thanks!"

"Put two dollars on Treehouse to show," he said.

Eddie made it to the window just before the betting closed. He placed his bet and jogged back to the rail just as the bugle called the horses to the post. Number seven shied, pawed the ground, and refused to enter his stall. Finally, he was in place and the gate sprang open.

The horses bolted out, and for the first quarter turn, they crowded together, a mass of brown and black, crimson, gold, purple, and green, moving as one. Then, they began to separate into twos and threes, and as their pounding hooves thundered by them, Eddie's heart was hammering. The smell of leather, fresh clods of earth, and straining horseflesh hit him like a powerful narcotic, and he was hooked.

This race was a short one, and by the time Treehouse flew by to place, Eddie was leaping up and down and pounding on the rail in excitement. Manny slapped him on the back. His ten-dollar payoff made Eddie feel almost light-headed. At the end of the second race, Eddie and Manny moved to seats higher up in the grandstands.

The jockeys entered the track on their mounts for the third race. Remembering the conversation he had overheard, Eddie mentioned the filly with the injured foreleg. Sure enough, number five, the chestnut mare favored to win, snorted and tossed her head every time she stepped on her left foot. Manny crossed her off his racing form in favor of a long shot called Danny Boy. Neither horse showed, but Manny had cut his losses, risking only twenty on the race.

By the finish of the fifth, Eddie was twenty dollars ahead and having the time of his life. Just prior to the start of the sixth race, a whisper like the sound of shuffling cards rippled through the crowd. Noticing the turning and craning heads of a group of spectators, Eddie squinted his eyes searching for the source of the commotion. Then he saw him. A familiar, short figure wearing a fedora had entered the stands accompanied by four bodyguards. People in the crowd pointed at him as he passed through heading for his private box. Expecting a comment of some sort, Eddie turned to look at Manny. Manny's jaw clenched, but he said nothing. If Manny had read the papers, he didn't seem surprised to see Capone out in public so soon after what had happened in Chicago.

The seventh race was approaching and African was running in a four-furlong heat.

"How much are you going to bet on him?" Eddie asked Manny.

"Nothing."

"Nothing?" Eddie knew he was the favorite and wouldn't pay big, but he was a sure thing.

"He won't win this one," Manny said, sounding certain.

They started for the window to place their bets. Intent on counting his money, Eddie had fallen a few paces behind. He didn't notice that Capone had left his box and was walking in their direction, heading right over to where they were standing. Just then, Eddie looked up. Capone had stopped short a few yards from them. He paused for a split second, and shot Eddie a confused look. He nodded at Manny but didn't speak. Manny quickly stepped back, letting Capone enter the line ahead of him. Eddie watched in amazement as he placed his bet.

He peeled seven hundred dollar bills off a huge roll and bet on Over Easy to win. The odds on Over Easy were eight to one.

After he had walked away, Manny nudged Eddie, leaned over and whispered in his ear.

"See that, Eddie? He never goes to the window himself. He always sends someone else to place his bets and collect his winnings. But today he wants to be sure everybody sees him."

Eddie was surprised to see Manny place his bet on Over Easy. Eddie put all his winnings on African to win. After his earlier successes, he felt he could pick a winner.

The bell clanged and the horses sprinted out of the post. African held a firm lead until the final turn. When the horses entered the stretch, African's jockey appeared to shift his position almost imperceptibly, and they fell back to second, then third place. By the time they crossed the finish line, they had dropped to fourth position, failing even to show, and Over Easy had nosed out number eight to win. Eddie's heart sank. He looked up to Capone's box seat. He was grinning, and he and his men were slapping each other on the back. Capone lit up a cigar and sat back down, this time sending one of his men to the window to collect his winnings.

Avoiding Eddie's eyes, Manny went to collect his own payoff, which was considerable. He had watched Eddie lose everything he had won that day. After the seventh race they left. On the way home Manny handed him another ten-dollar bill.

"Come on, Eddie." he said, "Don't take it personal. It's just the way life is."

*   *   *

Twenty-Two

On Thursday, the third month anniversary of her moving in, Diana suggested they take in an afternoon movie to celebrate the occasion.

"It will do you good to get out for a change," she insisted over Ed's objections.

They both agreed the spy film they saw was very good, and Ed had to admit that he had enjoyed the outing. On the way home, they decided to stop for a take-out meal at Joe's Crab Shack.

Earlier in the day, Ed had been feeling quite energetic. Before they left the house, he had puttered around the garage straightening his tools, but by the time they returned home from the theater and sat down to eat, he felt a wave of fatigue wash over him. He put down his fork.

"I guess all the activity today has worn me out. I can't seem to finish all this food," he apologized pushing his plate back. "If you don't mind, I think I'll just take my coffee into the living room and watch the news."

Diana was putting away the last of the dishes when a sharp clatter and the sound of breaking glass came from the living room.

"Oops, do you need a paper towel?" she called from the kitchen.

He tried to answer her but his mouth refused to form the words.

"Hang don wok."

"What?" she said coming into the living room. A shattered mug and spreading puddle of coffee lay on the floor at his feet.

"Ma hang." His tongue tangled the words.

"Dad? Are you all right?" she said. "Your eye looks funny."

He fixed her with his open eye, blinked it rapidly then looked down at his lap. With his left hand, he slapped at his right, which lay curled in his lap like a dead bird.

"Oh God," Diana gasped, dropping the dishtowel and rushing for the phone.

When the paramedics arrived, he was still sitting in his chair. Diana knelt next to him holding his left hand and murmuring soft, reassuring words.

"We'll take over now, Ma'am," one of EMTs said, setting up a folding gurney next to the chair. As one cradled his back and one his knees, the two attendants lifted his slight frame and carefully transferred him onto the gurney. Under the sheet, his body looked small and vulnerable.

Weaving in and out of traffic, Diana managed to keep up with the ambulance. She mouthed a silent Hail Mary.

"No. Not now," she whispered, "not today."

When the red lights swerved into the emergency entrance at the hospital, she followed them in and parked in a disabled slot near the door. She rushed inside just in time to see them wheeling him into a treatment room.

The four minutes it took for an ER doctor to arrive seemed like an eternity. Unable to stay still, she paced back and forth between the bed and the doorway until the young resident on duty finally walked in.

"You're Mr. Boyd's daughter? I'm Dr. Emelda Lopez," she said, touching Diana's shoulder. "It appears your father may have had a stroke. I want to get an MRI right away to see exactly how severe it is. It will take about half an hour. In the meantime, there are some forms that need to be filled out." She smiled and directed Diana toward the check-in desk.

After the paperwork was complete, Diana sat alone in the cubicle, her gaze wandering from the banks of sophisticated monitoring equipment to the clock on the wall and back again. Two hours had dragged by before they wheeled him back into the examining room. He seemed more alert, and although one side of his face still drooped, he tried to smile at her.

The waiting resumed. His eyes were closed, and he appeared to be sleeping. She continued her pacing, a gesture as unavoidable and ineffectual as repeatedly punching an elevator button hoping it will come. An hour later, the doctor reappeared.

"Well, the good news is that it was a small, localized bleed and appears to have stopped. Other than some temporary weakness on the right side, he should make a complete recovery," she said. "The bad news is that I can't give you a timetable for that. And at his age another stroke is a possibility you should be aware of."

At those words, Diana looked over at him. Ed's unaffected eye was fully open now and fixed intently on the doctor's face. His expression clearly registered his understanding of the doctor's final statement. Diana wiped a streak of moisture from the corner of his eye.

"We'll admit him now," Dr. Lopez went on, "but it'll be a while before a room is ready. You can go home if you like. They'll call you when he's settled, and you can bring his things—robe, shaving gear. Whatever will make him more comfortable."

When Diana returned an hour and a half later, they had moved him to a room on the second floor. The light was off, and Ed was snoring softly. The nurse at the desk left her post and stuck her head into the room.

"He's had a light sedative and will likely sleep for several hours," she said. "He's stable now, and you look as if you could use some rest," she continued. "Why don't you go home and get some sleep?"

Diana returned to the car and slumped down on the front seat. She hammered the steering wheel with her palms. She hadn't cried for years, not even through her separation and divorce. But now she couldn't seem to stop. All those years when she hadn't missed him at all seemed so long ago. Now, more than anything, she wanted him to be okay.

When she returned to the hospital the next morning, Diana found him propped up in bed. From his window, he could see the water of the bay. A different nurse was spooning lime Jello into his mouth and deftly recapturing the green drool that slipped out and dribbled down his chin.

"Hi," the nurse said cheerfully. "He had a good night. Slept like a top. The good news is that even though he's having a little trouble keeping food in his mouth, he's not having any difficulty swallowing. That's good because it means the paralysis is less serious than it looked at first. He's even regaining some movement in his arm."

"Ay," he said to Diana, smiling and wiggling the fingers on his right hand. The right side of his face had improved considerably, even though the corner of his mouth still drooped a little. She leaned over and kissed his cheek.

The next two weeks passed slowly. During the long rests between his rehab sessions, Diana kept him company. Within two days, he was walking with the help of a walker, and other than a slight slur, his speech had returned to normal. With little else to occupy him between his various therapies, he tried to pick up the thread of his story. Once, when the nurse attempted to force him to break off his narrative to rest his throat, he became frustrated and testy, even snapping at the pretty Candy Striper who brought him the morning paper. His eyes spoke the fear he wouldn't speak: who would finish the story if he died? As Diana sat beside his bed holding his hand, idly pulling her thumb over the tissue-thin skin, she read his thoughts but kept silent.

He took a sip of water. Looking toward the bay outside his window with a sigh, he cleared his throat and began where he had left off.

PART THREE

Pelican Justice

TWENTY-THREE

"It was after that day at the track," Ed mused, "that everything changed. Manny wasn't his old self anymore. He seemed more and more preoccupied. Even when he laughed, it sounded brittle, forced. With the newspapers all so full of scary economic predictions, and with so much concern about a coming crisis, I thought that was the cause of his moodiness. Everyone was concerned, so why not Manny? At least that's what I assumed at the time." Ed looked out toward the bay, opening a shuttered window into the past. "It was sometime in March. The days were getting longer. I remember the slant of the light over the water," he began.

*   *   *

After making their pickups, Manny and Eddie would sometimes linger a while on a bench near the bay front before parting for the afternoon. The return of the fishing boats was heralded by flocks of pelicans that fought for position on the many barnacle-covered posts lining the fishing pier. Like hounds, they waited patiently to retrieve the fish heads and guts thrown overboard by the fishermen as they cleaned their catch.

A big fishing boat was just pulling in. The captain cut the engine and eased the trawler in to the pier. As the two deck hands looped the fore and aft lines around the dock posts, the eager birds sailed off their perches into the water and circled about. As soon as the boat was secured, the captain and crew opened the locker in the rear where the fish were kept iced down and began unloading the day's catch. That day's haul was a good one: eight or ten large red snapper, several big bluefish, four grouper that were well over twenty-pounds each and miscellaneous smaller fish, mostly yellowtails and pompano. Each fish had to be gutted before it could be sold. The men accomplished this task with speed and precision, tossing the entrails and heads out into the water where the pelicans would rush in to claim a prize. Small fish circled fighting over the smaller pieces that sank below the surface.

Manny was particularly quiet that day, sitting slumped over with his elbows resting on his knees and staring at the drama being played out in the water. Finally he murmured softly, as if talking to himself.

"You think, hey, they're just a bunch of birds. They're all the same, right? Wrong. They got personalities just like people. See that guy over there—the one with all the scars on his head? He's the boss. Watch what happens when the scraps hit the water." He turned toward Eddie, a frown forcing his eyebrows together.

Those guts alone would be enough to satisfy the daily diet of a pelican aggressive enough to grab the lion's share. The pelican Manny had pointed out to Eddie was first to reach the boat. When any other birds attempted to enter his territory, he paddled toward them, pecking and flapping furiously. Eddie watched the scarred one gobble up more than half the fish guts, leaving the other eight or ten birds to fight over the rest.

"See?" Manny said. "As long as he's strong enough to keep his position, he's the boss and he doesn't have to work like the others. Those scars mean he's been top dog a long time."

They watched a while longer. Scarhead had snapped up a huge fish head and was trying to swallow it. It was apparently too big to go down, but he wasn't about to give it up. Several other birds approached, ready to fight over anything he spit out. Scarhead flapped his wings and tried to fly back to his post with his prize, but with his heavy load he couldn't get airborne and could only manage to hop clumsily over the surface of the water. Eddie could see that a cruising shark in the right place at the right time would probably someday make an easy meal of him.

Manny had retreated into himself again.

"You Okay?" Eddie asked.

"Well, maybe so and maybe not," he said in a tone that made Eddie feel uneasy. He looked back out to sea with a far-away, almost sad expression.

"There's something I've got to tell you, Eddie," he finally said.

"Okay," Eddie said and waited for him to go on.

For a long time, he didn't speak. He continued to stare out toward the horizon, and Eddie could see the muscles of his jaw twitching beneath the tan skin of his face.

"I have to . . ." he hesitated. He cleared his throat. "I have something for you," he said, looking back at Eddie with a rueful smile. He unbuckled the alligator band on his left wrist and removed his watch. Reaching over, he fastened it around Eddie's arm.

"This is for you. You know we can't afford for you to keep being late. You never know what time it is. Now you'll always be able to keep your appointments."

Eddie looked at the watch then back at Manny. He swallowed hard.

"And speaking of appointments, I have one right now," Manny said. He got up slowly, as if he were suddenly very tired.

"I'll see you, Eddie," he said and turned away.

Whatever Manny had wanted to tell him had gone unsaid. It hung in the air, like a cloud blotting out the sun. But there were no clouds in the sky that day, and the late afternoon light cast an orange glow on Manny's back as he followed his long shadow down the walk.

Eddie lingered there for a few minutes, looking out toward the water. The dock was deserted now. The crowd of rowdy pelicans had retired to their respective posts to digest the scraps in their fat craws and await the next incoming boat.

The sun was getting low now, and Eddie got up to leave. He was just crossing behind the bench to the path when a pale scrap of paper caught his attention. A creased envelope lay next to the rusty iron bench leg in a sandy patch of weedy ground. He reached down and picked it up.

Turning it over, he inspected the stained, worn paper which appeared to have been folded and refolded many times. It was still sealed, and across the front someone had written "addressee unknown." Eddie looked at the cramped scrawl:

Mrs. Wanda Silver
28 Sandy Shore Drive
Chicago, Illinois

It must have fallen from Manny's pocket. Eddie sat back down. He held the envelope for a long time, nervously running his thumbnail under a loose edge of the sealed flap. Finally he held it up to the light. Through the thin envelope, he could make out only a few words.

". . . that you can give . . . promise you . . . together"

He stared at it for another moment or two and then reverently refolded the fragile envelope and placed it back where he had found it. He felt a little ashamed, as if merely by touching it he might have reopened an unhealed wound in Manny that he had not meant to hurt.

A mockingbird warbled in a distant tree. Although these birds never repeated the same tune, there was something, a subtle tone or lilt, which differentiated a morning from an evening call. Just before nightfall, there was a sweeter, almost mournful quality to their song. The sound reminded Eddie that it was getting late, and he stood up and turned toward home.

Twenty-four

For several days, Eddie thought back to that unopened letter and Manny's parting comment. There had been nothing unusual about the words. "I'll see you, Eddie," he had said, as he'd said so many times before. But this time there had been something about his tone that left Eddie feeling uncertain and a little scared.

For nearly a week, Eddie wandered from one to another of their new meeting places hoping to find him, but Manny wasn't anywhere. Eddie had stayed away from the sandwich shop, but finally, curiosity overcame caution and he decided that maybe it wouldn't hurt to wander over and see if Manny had returned to the place of their first meeting. He walked toward the back of the shop and began browsing through a magazine, all the while keeping one eye on the door. A low whisper behind him tickled the hair behind his ear and sent an icy chill through him.

"If you're looking for who I think you are, don't be wasting your time. He isn't here. And another thing," the voice said, "the word on the street is that he's had someone working with him. Certain people are trying to find out who this someone is. It's not like I didn't warn you about that, but you didn't listen. If I was you, I'd watch my back."

Eddie spun around to see Capone's driver Frank moving away from him toward the door. He tried to say something, but his throat was filled with sandpaper. He watched until he was sure Frank had gone then collapsed against the shelf, sending a whole pile of newspapers tumbling to the floor.

In less than ten seconds, all Eddie's naïve dreams of the easy life had evaporated with the cold sweat on his forehead. He was left with a silent vacuum inside that for all its emptiness felt as heavy as an anchor. He sprinted toward home. He was so preoccupied with his thoughts that when he arrived at his doorstep he had no memory of how he had gotten there.

He knew he was in big trouble. He spent several sleepless nights shaking every time the wind rattled the shutters. He was sure they were coming for him. While lying in sleepless terror one night, he came up with a plan that might get him out of sight, for a while at least.

He and Jim had explored some islands in the bay several summers ago when they had a small sailboat. The sandy plots, covered with palms, sea grapes, and other low vegetation, had been totally deserted. One of these might provide him a place to hide without alerting his parents to the serious mess he had gotten himself into. Easter vacation was less than a week away.

That afternoon he went to see Jim. It had been a long while since they'd spent much time together. If Jim was surprised at the sudden visit, he didn't comment. Eddie set to work trying to sell him on the idea of the two of them spending their Easter vacation camping out on one of the islands. An obvious problem was that neither of them had a boat now.

"How are we supposed to get there? Walk on water?" Jim frowned.

"We'll figure something out," Eddie tried enthusiastically. "That'll be part of the fun."

Desperation is often a powerful source of inspiration, and by the time Eddie had finished his presentation, he was tired, but Jim was convinced.

Their parents approved their plan to camp out, happy to see the boys were spending time together again, and by early the next Saturday they had built two makeshift boats using galvanized washtubs and inner tubes. The tubs cradled inside the inner tubes were stable and had enough carrying capacity to hold their provisions. Jim had managed to talk his mother out of a frying pan and a stew pot, a sack of potatoes, and some canned goods from their kitchen to carry in his boat. Eddie stocked his with an old tarp to use as a tent, two bedrolls, their two rifles, and fishing gear. Fresh water was their heaviest cargo, and they split it between the two of them. They borrowed an old wheelbarrow from Jim's next-door neighbor and hauled their things down to the water hoping their boats would float. Once assured they would, they waded out from shore.

Holding on to the tubes, they pushed off, kicking and paddling. They steered toward the islands that appeared as just tiny specks on the horizon from where they had set out. Once they reached deeper water, Eddie began to worry that their kicking would attract sharks. He knew big tigers and hammerheads were common there.

"Can't you kick without splashing?" he snapped at Jim. He scanned the water around them.

"Just how do you expect to move if we don't kick?" Jim shot back.

Eddie worked at keeping his splashes to a minimum while trying to watch for large shapes or fins breaking the surface. After an exhausting hour of paddling and kicking, their feet finally touched the grassy bottom. The shallows surrounding the island were a breeding ground for spiny sea urchins. Eddie and Jim had both stepped on them often enough to know that a broken-off spine lodged in the sole of the foot was extremely painful and could easily become infected. The only remedy was soaking the foot in urine, which would eventually dissolve the calciferous spine. They picked their way carefully through the minefield of urchins and finally dragged their boats up on the sand.

After resting on the beach to catch their breath, they set to work cutting saplings to support their makeshift tent. That completed, they stored their supplies and opened a can of soup.

"Jeez, Jim, couldn't you get more food? This soup won't last us long," Eddie complained.

"Hey, Eddie, I was lucky to get this much. Besides, we can make more soup with our potato peelings. My old man told me that's how the Krauts survived during the war."

Darkness fell, and a full moon rose out of the ocean. The night was clear. Directly over their heads, the Milky Way shone in the sequined blackness like a dusty path through the star-shot sky. A light breeze rustled the palm fronds overhead. The only other sound was the soft murmur of waves lapping at the sandy shore. As they lay down to enjoy the perfect tropical night, Eddie was able to draw his first easy breath in days. Exhaustion from the day's exertions soon overcame them, and they stripped down to their underwear and in no time were both asleep.

Sometime in the night, they awoke simultaneously. The air had become deadly still, and thousands of no-see-ums had descended upon them in a feeding frenzy. They thrashed around the tent alternately cursing and slapping at the invisible enemy that had settled on every bare expanse of skin.

"Jesus, Mary and Joseph! I can't stand these damned things," Jim croaked. "I gotta get out of here!"

Dashing from the tent, they streaked toward the water and waded in up to their necks. They were forced to stay there until nearly dawn, when a breeze started up again and the stinging pests disappeared. Jim griped about his interrupted sleep, and Eddie tried to cajole him out of his irritable mood. It seemed to him a small price to pay for his peace of mind.

The next day was better, and they spent most of it swimming, fishing and acquiring third-degree burns. Although they had counted on their fishing skills to supplement their diet, fish proved to be quite scarce, other than the plentiful blowfish that lived around the coral outcroppings in the shallow water. Three out of every four fish they caught were blowfish. Considering them inedible, they threw them back. When they got hungry, though, they began to reconsider.

"Bahamian fishermen say if you are careful not to puncture the guts, you can cut the tail off and eat it," said Jim. "Think we should try it?"

"I don't know," Eddie warned. "Mr. Mouskouri told me they're poisonous. He says if that green bladder breaks and leaks on the meat, it can kill you."

Hunger finally won out, and although it took many tails to make a meal, they were pretty tasty.

Eddie was now sleeping better at night, but when a motorized boat approached the island one afternoon, he ducked into the tent, grabbed his rifle and waited to come out until it was gone.

"What's wrong, Eddie?" Jim wanted to know. "I've never seen you so jumpy!"

"Nothing. Just . . . uh, someone might be looking for me."

Jim looked at him questioningly, waiting for him to continue. Eddie remained silent.

"What? Who's looking for you? Why?" Jim persisted, waiting for an answer. But Eddie just continued to hold his gun at the ready. Jim didn't press him for more details. He recognized Eddie's reaction and the silence as unspoken testimony to his fear. Eddie's taut stillness made Jim feel afraid for him.

On their fourth day on the island, they looked up from their fishing to see a fast-approaching boat heading in their direction. They scrabbled frantically back to the tent, grabbed their rifles and then took cover behind a thick screen of sea grape bushes. The boat beached in the soft sand, and a laughing couple slipped over the side. The man helped his companion into the shallow water, and peeling off their swimsuits, they ran up the beach. Eddie knew what they had in mind.

"I'll bet that sunburn she's got won't feel too good when she's lying on her back in the sand," he said.

From their vantage point behind the bushes they watched as the couple satisfied themselves with great athleticism. When they had finished, they rolled onto their backs panting for several minutes. Then they rose, picked up their swimsuits, and waded into the water to wash the grit off each other before putting them back on. After they dressed, they settled back on the hard-packed sand at the water's edge laughing and talking, seemingly in no hurry to leave.

Now that the show was over, Eddie and Jim were anxious to leave their cramped hiding place and stretch their legs. To their relief, the couple finally got up and climbed back into their boat. They headed out into the bay, and Eddie and Jim resumed fishing.

Since they had come to the island, Eddie had been feeling uncomfortable and guilty for subjecting Jim to danger without his even being aware of it. Eddie silently weighed the pros and cons of letting Jim in on his secret and decided he'd tell him everything. He had never kept anything from Jim before he met Manny. And there might be some benefit to confiding in him. He yearned to unburden himself of the weight he'd been bearing alone. Jim could be a more objective judge of the situation he'd gotten himself into and perhaps help him sort things out.

That night they lay in the tent joking about the couple they had seen that afternoon. Eddie decided to ease into his confession, beginning with a trivial comment meant to get Jim's attention.

"She wasn't a real blonde. You know how I know?" he said.

"Huh?" Jim mumbled sleepily.

"That girl on the beach today. She wasn't a real blonde."

Jim's only reply was a soft snore.

"Never mind," Eddie said and closed his eyes. The moment had been lost.

As the next two days passed, Eddie tried to convince himself that his fears were overblown. Frank had probably made up the part about them looking for Manny's accomplice just to scare him, although he had to admit it had worked pretty well.

Soon, he and Jim knew they had sadly underestimated their fresh water requirements, and even with rationing and some extra water they had caught in their pans during a hard rain, they had nearly run out. They left the island a day earlier than they had planned. Sunburned, hungry and thirsty, Eddie was tired and looking forward to getting back to regular meals and a soft bed. But the heaviness that had settled into his bones and weighed him down was more than just the usual fatigue following a week of camping.

TWENTY-FIVE

At the end of vacation Eddie went back to school, and although he had always been quiet, he was even more somber and serious than usual. His stomach felt full of nails, and he lost his taste even for donuts. He found it impossible to concentrate, and more and more often he couldn't answer even the simplest questions in class. Father Horka noticed the change and stepped up to him one day as he was collecting his books at the end of the period.

"Hey, Eddie," he said. "You haven't dropped in for a visit in a while. What about a chat? Come by my office this afternoon?"

Later that day as Eddie raised his hand to knock at the scarred office door, he examined the worn wood. Every nick and scratch was as familiar to him as the freckles on back of his own hand. He had actually spent a lot of time in that room. With its overstuffed bookcases and well-worn furniture, it radiated a warm coziness that Eddie had found inviting. Until he met Manny, he had come here two or three afternoons a week to borrow books and talk about history.

"Come in," a muffled voice called from the other side of the door. Father looked up when he entered. "Oh, Eddie, you've come. Good."

"Yes, Father," he said, standing stiffly by the door.

"Well, come on in and sit down," Father Horka said, gesturing to an easy chair.

"So, what have you been up to lately?" he said.

"Nothing."

Eddie perched on the chair's big padded arm and rested his satchel in the seat. He didn't intend to stay long enough to sit down.

"Really."

It had been a statement, not a question, but he looked at Eddie, smiling, inviting him to continue. Eddie's silence elicited a shrug.

"Well, if you say so," he said. "I notice your visits to the confessional have been scarce as hen's teeth lately. You don't want to wait too long. Sins have a way of accumulating, and they can really weigh down a person's soul like a huge stone he has to lug around."

Eddie squirmed and reached for his satchel.

"This world is precarious enough today, and there's a lot we can't control," Father went on. "Look at the economy. Then there's some pretty dangerous characters in Europe we've got to watch out for—we've just got to hope for the best. But luckily, the health of our soul, Eddie, is something entirely in our hands. And God's, of course. You're only a year from graduation now. Have you thought of what you'll do then? Given any thought to college?"

"Not college, Father. I've been thinking about getting a job. Maybe with the new airline."

"You'll want to keep your mind on your studies if you hope to do that," he responded.

"Yes, Father," Eddie said, wiping beads of sweat from his upper lip. "I know I haven't been the best student lately."

"How's your attendance been? I've been meaning to ask."

"I'm in English every day, Father," he said looking at his feet.

"And what do you do in the afternoon?"

"I like to fish." Eddie's eyes darted around the room. Not a lie exactly, but surely an equivocation. He was getting more adept at this form of deception, but not so much that he didn't feel a twinge pulling at his conscience.

"Well, fishing is fine, but it won't get you anything but fish. Think about that, Eddie. And I don't really believe you came to see me today to talk about fishing. If you decide you want to visit about what's really bothering you, come back. The door is always open."

Eddie's thoughts were pulling him in two directions when he left Father Horka's office. He spent the rest of that week trying to keep his worry safely hidden behind a weak smile. But when he picked up *The Herald* on Friday morning, he was stunned. There on the front page, the face of James Alderman stared back at him. In the mug shot, the red-haired rumrunner looked harder and more frightening than he had in person. Eddie felt something shift in the pit of his stomach. The smiling man with the big teeth he had seen with Manny couldn't be the same Alderman glaring out from under a headline proclaiming him guilty of the murder of two Coast Guardsmen and a Secret Service operative in a bloody gun battle!

According to the article, Alderman and an accomplice had been chased down and caught bringing in a load of rum, but not before Alderman had managed to shoot and kill three men in the chase boat. All the details of the capture at sea were described in a narrative that read like a thriller. The article made him sound almost heroic. Eddie nervously picked at a callous on his finger as he tore through the lurid details of the chase and arrest.

Manny's disappearance had been worrisome enough, and now the capture of Alderman added another knot to the rope tightening around his gut. For the next few weeks, he stayed far away from all his former pick-up points, knowing someone would surely be watching for him, waiting to grill him about Manny's whereabouts. He found it impossible to control his imagination, which kept replaying in growing detail what they might do to get him to tell what he didn't know.

This was a burden he still carried alone. He had tried to tell Jim back on the island when the time seemed right, but he had let the opportunity slip by. Even though he knew that whatever he might reveal in the confessional was privileged, he couldn't bring himself to admit more details of his sinful double life to Father Horka. Day after day he worried in silence, trying to ignore the worm of guilt crawling around in his belly, eating him up by slow degrees. He had to find out where Manny was.

One day, he couldn't bear it any longer. He just had to talk to someone. Eddie went to Junior's stand.

"You seen Big Manny around?" he asked him.

"Naw, Eddie. You?"

"No. I just thought . . ." Eddie trailed off, not knowing what else to say.

"I don't think we gonna see Mr. Manny 'round here for a long space of time neither," Junior whispered. "Sho'ly is too bad too. That man had a lots'a shoes, and he always tipped real good. I'm sho gonna miss him."

When Eddie left the arcade, it had begun to rain. Dark thunderheads had been building all morning, and now heavy and low, the clouds had opened up, wrapping the city in a wet gray shroud. He walked home slowly, letting the sky pour down on him.

Estelle had agreed to meet Eddie the next day at their usual jitney stop. Because it had rained for the last three days and more was predicted, they had decided to take in a matinee together rather than going to the beach. They both wanted to see *Blackmail*, a thriller by a new director named Hitchcock.

When Eddie set out that morning, it was pouring. He had to walk several blocks to meet Estelle and was nearly soaked by the time he got to their corner. As he waited, the downpour slowed to occasional spatters of fat drops that fell intermittently through a light curtain of drizzle. The thick canopy of a big Poinciana tree on the corner provided a fairly dry spot to wait, and Eddie huddled against the trunk watching for Estelle. He wondered if she'd decided to cancel their outing because of the weather.

Across the street from where he stood, three little boys pretending to be Indians were dancing around in a mud puddle. They had painted their faces and bare chests with mud and were whooping and twirling like braves on the warpath. The dance quickly deteriorated into a water fight when one dancer began stomping and kicking muddy water on the others who gleefully reciprocated. The three were soon wet as seals and laughing hysterically. Eddie watched them. Although they were only a few years younger, it seemed a lifetime since he had felt so free. A damp breeze ruffled the leaves above his head, sending cascades of spent, orange-colored blossoms swirling through the air like confetti.

When he looked back up the street, he saw a red and white striped umbrella bobbing toward him. Although he couldn't see a face, he recognized the long shapely legs and lit up inside like the sun had just come out. The sprinkle of freckles on her cheeks and the smell of her hair always brought a flush to Eddie's face. By the time she reached the corner, it had almost stopped raining, and Estelle paused to collapse her umbrella. When she spotted him standing under the tree, she smiled and hurried over to him and planted a kiss on his cheek.

"I was afraid you might not come," he said.

"You thought I'd miss a picture show?" she teased.

The rain had begun to fall again, and they walked toward Flagler Street huddled together under her umbrella. Estelle was quieter today than usual; she concentrated on avoiding the puddles that had collected in depressions in the street and sidewalk. Eddie followed her lead and said little, content just to be next to her and feel the warmth of the small of her back under his palm.

Eddie wanted to delay getting to the theater until the last minute in order to avoid seeing anyone they might know waiting in line. There would probably be a crowd today. *Blackmail* had been made both as a silent film and a talky. The Olympia Theater was recently wired for sound, and everyone was excited about seeing the new version. When they reached the box office, only two people were still in line waiting to purchase tickets.

Eddie paid for theirs, and they entered the lobby. Estelle paused to walk around the theater's elegant interior. It was designed to look like an exotic Moorish palace with elaborately carved arches, gilt wall sconces, and cobalt blue and gold tiled benches. Inside the theater, the high ceiling was side-lit with blue lights to look like an evening sky, and tiny lights sprinkled the deep cobalt canopy, simulating stars. The picture was about to begin, and they hurried toward the stairway leading to the balcony. They took their seats just as the curtains opened.

The picture was a technical disaster, and the audience hooted and booed loudly to proclaim their disappointment. At times the film seemed pieced together, with long periods of nothing but sound effects. Other awkward scenes showed the actors with their backs to the camera. This had been done so dialogue could be dubbed in over the original silent scenes without having to synchronize the actors' lips with the sound. There were even different actors playing some of the bit parts. The neighbor who described how she found the body was played by one actress in one scene and by another actress in a later scene. That was really confusing. At the movie's end, the murderess got away with the crime.

The rain had let up by the time they left the theater.

"That was a dumb movie," Eddie said. "She was asking for trouble going to the artist's studio to begin with. And if she killed him in self-defense, why should she be afraid to confess? She probably didn't confess because she felt guilty for getting involved with a guy like that to begin with."

"Well, she did try to confess," Estelle reminded him. "Sometimes it just isn't so simple. Maybe she realized that confessing wouldn't change anything, couldn't bring him back, so she just went on with her life."

They had walked two blocks when Estelle stopped and turned toward him. She looked at Eddie intently, as if trying to read something in his face.

"What?" he asked her.

"Eddie, I've been meaning to tell you something, but I just couldn't find the right time. I can't put it off any longer," she began slowly. Without meeting his eyes she said, "I'm going back to Tallahassee. I got a letter from my father. I guess things didn't work out for him and his new wife. He wants me to come home."

Eddie's heart dropped like a sinker. "Do you want to go?"

"I guess so . . . I mean he's all the family I have. Everyone needs a family, don't you think? Maybe things will work out better now."

"But there's something else, Eddie," she added. "I've heard things . . . about Manny . . . I think you should know. I've heard talk that he's dropped out of sight. He's been playing both ends against the middle, and now he's in trouble. I thought I should tell you," she said, taking his hand. "I'm leaving here, Eddie, going back to another place and a different life. But this is your home. Now that Manny's not around, this is your chance to go back to a regular life, a safe life. I'd hate for anything to happen to you, you know? She kissed him on the cheek, turned and slipped her hand into his. They walked the rest of the way in silence.

They said goodbye under the Poinciana tree.

"Promise me you'll think about what I said," she whispered.

"I will. Cross my heart," Eddie said making a mark over his chest.

She crossed to the other side of the street, deftly hopping over a large puddle. She turned and smiled at him one last time then hurried away. Eddie waved and watched her disappear into the hazy lights in the distance.

Twenty-six

Just a month after his capture, the authorities tried, convicted, and sentenced James Alderman to death by hanging, upholding his Constitutional right to a speedy trial. During his imprisonment, he had attracted a great public following. Most members of the community sympathized with him, and in a short time they had elevated him to the status of folk hero. After all, he was only delivering a commodity everyone wanted and enjoyed, and one that provided a very real boost to the economy. The fact that it was an illegal commodity seemed to bother no one. Few people had ever embraced the Eighteenth Amendment, either in principle or in reality. As always, the government's logic was rarely the logic of the masses. Furthermore, with people's growing sense of frustration with the government's failed attempts to bolster the flagging economy, Alderman was the closest thing they had to Robin Hood.

While Alderman sat in jail, though, he apparently had lots of time to think and to get right with God. He spent much of his time writing, and *The Miami Herald* provided a forum for his testimonials of redemption. Along with the numerous stories written by reporters covering the arrest and impending execution, *The Herald* published several of the prisoner's own letters.

The day following his hanging, the front page carried a detailed description of Alderman's last hours, his ascent up the scaffold steps and consequent hanging.

Along with it, the article included Alderman's death message. Eddie read it with the strange feeling of having known the message's writer.

> When this is read I will have passed over the brink of eternity into the Great Beyond.
>
> I would like to state through the medium of the Miami Herald that I am feeling fine physically, mentally and spiritually. With the wonderful comfort and strength that I received from Jesus Christ, I am assured that when tomorrow comes I will go with smiles of comfort on my face. I am only dying from a physical standpoint. I shall live on spiritually in that Great Beyond. I shall carry on in the new life which I have found in prison and that life can't be taken from me, since I have been born out of darkness into the spirit of the great Jesus Christ.
>
> As I sit here in my cell I can look back and see just what caused me to be where I am today. Drunkenness first starts a young man to gambling—and swearing grows on him—and from that step he becomes hardened in his heart in envy and hatred toward mankind. Then, as he grows up, he becomes what you would call educated to crime. Bootlegging and smuggling is the next step. And there are other angles of downfall that lead to the devil.

Eddie stopped reading and looked down at his hands. Alderman could be describing him. Gambling, swearing and bootlegging. Licking his dry lips, he returned to the article.

> The money I made did neither me nor my dear family any good. We thought it did, but no. You can see what it has done—a death sentence by hanging—and a broken-hearted family. And I

wanted the public to know just how I feel about leaving this world
of sin and joining hands with the One that died on the Cross and
shed his blood for just such men as I was.

Eddie perused the front page of the paper, searching for more macabre details. According to the article, hundreds of people had gone to the funeral home to see his remains in the embalming room even before his body had been placed in his casket. After he was put out on display, the line of people who came to view him went on for most of the day. The reporter described him lying there in his casket, *"faintly smiling in the loneliness of death."*

Eddie thought of the descriptions of the Inferno and grimaced. This reporter obviously hadn't read Dante. With all those tortured souls writhing in the everlasting fire, Alderman would have plenty of company. And he certainly wouldn't be smiling.

The funeral was scheduled for three-thirty that afternoon with a viewing prior to the service. Eddie had never been to a Protestant church and was curious to know what a funeral for a criminal would be like. He decided to leave school early to go see it for himself. He talked Jim into coming with him. Although he said it was a creepy idea, he agreed to go.

Eddie and Jim arrived at the Alliance Tabernacle a few minutes after three and stood for a while outside with the crowd waiting to enter the church. When people began to file toward the doors, Eddie made no move to join them.

"Well, what are we waiting for?" Jim asked.

Eddie heard Father Horka's voice echoing in his head, warning of the perils of going into a Protestant church. Worrying that his soul would be in trouble if he went in, he paced back and forth busy calculating the severity of the sin he might be committing.

"It's just that this isn't a Catholic church," Eddie finally said, feeling a little foolish.

"Oh, come on, that's a lot of baloney. Besides, that's what confession is for." Jim turned and started up the steps.

Eddie quickly made up his mind and followed him into the dark sanctuary. Against the far wall, between two windows, the casket sat on a platform surrounded by an enormous bank of flowers. The chapel was dimly lit by electric lights and was stiflingly hot. The two large ceiling fans and one wall fan did little but circulate the steamy mixture of odors—flowers, sweaty bodies, women's perfume, and burning candles—and provide a droning undertone to the whispers of the crowd of onlookers. For a minute, Eddie thought he might lose his lunch.

They joined the line of mourners and curiosity seekers who moved slowly forward to get a look at the deceased. The line would stop periodically every time someone at the front knelt at the casket to offer a prayer, and during these pauses Eddie looked around at the diverse array of individuals who had gathered here.

Some of the men were dressed like laborers; others, wearing expensive suits, looked like prosperous members of the business community. In the church that day the boys saw the old and young, women and children, some who seemed truly saddened, and others, the two of them included, who gawked at the goings-on like spectators at a circus.

A man several yards in front of them lifted a little boy onto his shoulders so he could see over the heads of the crowd.

"Daddy, why ain't the man in the box sweatin'?" he piped in a shrill voice.

His father shushed him and lowered him back to the floor.

Finally, Eddie and Jim reached the front of the line. There was Alderman laid out in his casket. On the inside of the lid was a plaque with the inscription "James Horace Alderman". He was dressed in a summer suit, orchid bowtie and a matching handkerchief tucked into his breast pocket.

Eddie leaned in over his face, which had been made up with some sort of thick, waxy concoction that could have filled a crack a mile wide. Alderman was smiling, just as the reporter had said. Not a big grin; just a tasteful little upturn of the lips—obviously another bit of undertaker's magic.

After they passed the casket, they decided they'd seen enough. When the line neared a side door, they exited into the bright sunlight. Jim was squinting, shading his eyes and peering at Eddie.

"When you leaned over him, I was afraid you were going to kiss him or something!"

Eddie snorted derisively.

"I just wanted to see if the rope left a mark on his neck. It didn't, or if it did, the make-up must have covered it."

"Jeez, I hope when I die they don't lay me out smiling. That's just plain weird," Jim concluded with a shiver.

Twenty-seven

On the morning after the funeral, Eddie's eggs sat on the breakfast table untouched and cold while he paged through the newspaper with a grim foreboding. Day after day, the worsening financial situation was heralded in bold, four-inch headlines. Every article, it seemed, forecast a complete and long-lasting collapse of the economy.

Still, his father didn't seem too worried. His job appeared secure; in fact, he'd been busier than ever. He had received a call late the day before from the paper sending him downtown to cover an increasingly familiar story. Eddie overheard just enough of the conversation to conclude that a jumper had leapt from the top floor of the courthouse.

This new casualty must have been someone of great importance. Upon hearing the news, Eddie's father whispered, "Jesus H. Christ!" The commandment against blasphemy was not casually broken in their home, at least not in Eddie's mother's presence, and she shot him a withering look when he hung up the telephone. Without stopping to explain, he grabbed his equipment and hurried out the door.

Hours later when he came home, he looked drawn and was unusually quiet. Eddie followed him into the kitchen.

"Who was it? How many stories did he fall?"

His father stared out the window and let the questions remain answered. Clearly, despite his outward show of confidence, even he was beginning to feel some of the black mood of despair that had befallen everyone.

Every day, Eddie hoped for some indication that the crisis was just a temporary economic setback and would soon blow away like a sudden squall. Every day seemed worse than the last, though, with no end in sight. If the most pessimistic reports were true, Armageddon was just around the corner.

When his father announced three weeks later that they would be moving, Eddie's stomach dropped to his feet. For months, he had been dreading this moment. He had known that it was just a matter of time before their luck, too, would turn. He sat very still waiting for the other announcement that would surely follow—the cheery news that he was to be pulled out of school. When his father didn't speak, Eddie looked up to see him smiling.

"What? What's funny?"

"Well, wait till you see," Mr. Boyd said, smiling enigmatically. His mother was smiling too.

"Let's go see the house," he said to Eddie. "Come on, we can walk there."

Eddie shoved his chair back too abruptly and reached out to catch it just before it toppled backward. What was wrong with their house? He imagined the new place. It would probably be much smaller than their present one. It would also likely be nearer the seedy section east of their neighborhood, maybe right near The Greentree Hotel. How could they spring this awful news on him and then casually smile about it?

Their route took them a block over toward the bay and then west toward Seventeenth Avenue. His father ignored him, refusing to comment when Eddie shoved his hands deep into his pockets and scowled sullenly. His father had told him the new house wasn't far from where they lived. That, at least, was good. As they continued on, the street numbers dropped and the size of the houses increased. He began to notice that the modest bungalows in his own neighborhood were shabby compared to these newer, grander places just a few blocks over. Some even had walled gardens and Moorish arched windows edged with brightly colored tiles.

His father stopped in front of a large, two-story home.

"Well, what do you think?" he asked. "How would you like to live here?"

Eddie looked over at him to see if he was joking.

"Well?" He paused. "If you don't like it . . ."

"No! It's really . . . big!" Eddie couldn't believe his eyes.

"Want to go inside?"

The house was huge by their standards, two stories with four bedrooms and two baths on the upper floor, a separate garage, and servants' quarters in the rear. Eddie wandered through the empty rooms not yet able to take it all in. He tried to imagine living here, his mother and the ladies in her bridge club laughing over coffee in the sun porch, his father reading his paper by the fireplace, and servants' quarters . . . suddenly he thought about Jim.

"Can I go see the servants' quarters?" he asked. Already he had visions of the two of them appropriating this outbuilding as their own private domain, where they could talk and make plans free from the prying ears and eyes of parents. He ran out to take a look.

A hedge of tall, neatly trimmed podocarpus bushes lined the drive leading to the garage in the rear. As Eddie came around the bend, he stopped dead in his tracks. A brand new Jaguar roadster sat parked in the driveway. The car was the most beautiful thing he had ever seen; it was a rich cream color, long and low with the same sleek profile as the cat ornament that adorned its hood. The top was down. Eddie approached it with the same respectful awe he felt for the statue of the Blessed Virgin in the sacristy at St. Joseph's. He looked around. No one was in sight. He had left his father inside measuring and planning where their furniture would fit. Quietly opening the car door, Eddie climbed into the beautifully appointed interior, running his hands lovingly over the warm, brown leather seats. The polished wood of the steering wheel and fittings shone in the sun. Eddie had never ever seen wood like this, but he could tell it was something exotic and expensive. This sleek machine even had a seventeen-jewel clock mounted in the dashboard.

The back door to the house suddenly slammed, startling Eddie out of his dream.

"Get out of that car, Eddie," his father snapped.

"Whose is it?" he asked.

"It's not ours."

When they got back home, his mother was waiting for them, obviously eager to see his reaction.

"Well? Isn't it wonderful?" she bubbled, dancing around like a schoolgirl.

"It's swell!" Eddie said. "I can't believe it. But how can we afford to move into a place like that?"

As his father explained, some of his joy evaporated. It seemed that in the midst of the current financial drought, the Boyds had stumbled onto an oasis. A few lucky people like them were able to benefit from the changing vicissitudes of the economy. When the unfortunate former owner jumped from the sixth floor of a downtown building after learning his entire portfolio of stocks was worthless, the Boyds had been at the right place at the right time to cash in on his bad luck. His bereaved family had been forced to move out leaving the property in foreclosure. The bank was happy to find an employed individual to rent it for a bargain price. The grieving widow had left her husband's expensive car behind feeling it might bring her further bad luck.

Eddie's father shared her superstitious misgivings. He instructed Eddie to leave the car, a reminder of the misfortune of the owner, right where it was. Eddie begged his father to reconsider, but he wouldn't budge, refusing to benefit further from the poor man's tragic demise.

Eddie couldn't do anything but watch, as day after day the car stood in the rain and the hot sun right where it had been left. His father refused even to move it into the garage. In a short time, the fine, supple leather seats cracked and the beautiful wood dashboard bleached out to a pale gray until the beautiful car gradually lost its appeal and became a monument to the sad times.

*   *   *

"So your family finally moved up in the world?" Diana asked, smiling. "That must have been wonderful."

"Well, the good luck didn't last long," Ed said with a sad smile. "It never did, but up to that time, I'd never lost anything that meant something to me. People all around us were losing everything, but not me. I was young, stupid and untouched."

Ed went on, "Mother, of course, wasted no time getting into the social scene. Cashing in on my father's good fortune, she immediately planned a big social function to introduce our newly elevated family into the neighborhood. She had Beatrice working day and night dusting and polishing for the first couple weeks. Then, just before the big event, she came to me. When she offered to pay me to gig some frogs for her popular frog leg hors d'oeuvres, I agreed. My money was pretty much gone by then, and with Manny and Estelle gone too, I was glad to have something to do."

*   *   *

Twenty-eight

Frog gigging was strictly a nighttime activity. The best place for finding frogs was about twenty miles west of the city out the Tamiami Trail. The bike ride alone would take about half a day, so Eddie planned to camp out over night. He dug his pup tent out of the closet, took it outside and gave it a vigorous shake before carefully inspecting it for any scorpions or centipedes that might still be lurking inside. He put the book he was reading and his lantern and gig inside the tent, rolled the whole thing into a tight bundle, and strapped it securely behind his bicycle seat. He prepared a bag of sandwiches, apples, a thermos of lemonade and a chocolate bar and secured it on top of his tent roll. It was a long haul, and he'd reward himself when he got there with part of his stash for lunch and save the rest for dinner.

He had asked Jim to come along, but he was busy so Eddie went alone. At another time, he might have tried to persuade him, tempting him with the promise of food; on this day, though, he didn't. This time, he welcomed the opportunity for solitude. After stoking his energy with a big breakfast, he was out of the house before his parents were up.

It was still early when he pulled his bike off the road and started down an overgrown path. He usually liked to hike back off the more traveled trails where the wildlife was more abundant. He never failed to spot water moccasins, alligators, turtles, herons, spoonbills, and bullfrogs, which were plentiful.

Eddie remembered that the last time he had been on this particular trail, he'd had the rare chance to witness natural selection at work when he came across a nest of alligator eggs just hatching. A large hawk had spotted the tender morsels and swooped in for an easy meal. Right then, the mother gator had appeared on the scene. She hauled herself up on the bank and rushed in to guard her babies. When aroused, an alligator can move with amazing speed. The hawk managed to grab one wriggling prize and was just about to fly off when, snap. Goodbye hawk. It didn't take more than a second for her to return to her nest to feed her hatchlings their first meal of blood and feathers. As he passed the same spot, he thought those babies must be several feet long by now.

This part of the Everglades was crisscrossed with an extensive network of catwalks built years earlier by the Seminole Indians and the swamp men who lived here. These cypress walkways meandered out over the shallow water, at one time connecting thatched dwellings, called chickees, to sparsely scattered islands of dry land. Although many of the wooden bridges still existed, most of the fragile chickees had fallen prey to the recent hurricane and had been blown away leaving only the remaining foundation poles sticking up above water.

Eddie found one walkway that was still relatively sturdy and followed it seventy-five yards or so into the saw grass looking for a spot where frogs were plentiful. He trained his eyes on the shadowy shallows at the base of the verge of saw grass running along one side of the catwalk.

These shady places were the favorite daytime hideouts for bullfrogs. The yellow-green dapple of filtered sunlight on the water resembled their mottled coloration and provided perfect camouflage. Usually, they would submerge themselves, leaving only their bulging eyes and nostrils above water to wait patiently for a dragonfly or grasshopper to come within reach of their sticky tongue. Eddie quickly spotted several large ones lying just beneath the surface within yards of where he stood.

He was satisfied that he'd be able to catch plenty of frogs right here along this stretch of walk and decided this was a promising place to pitch his tent. He unfolded the brown canvas and spread it out on the catwalk. After inserting poles at the door flap and back, he tied ropes at the four corners, looping them around the cypress posts and pulling them taut. Then he crawled inside to admire his handiwork.

He laid out the rest of his equipment: his lantern, gig, and an old pair of pajama pants that made a quite serviceable frog sack. They had a drawstring at the top and Eddie had knotted the leg bottoms. With his catch stuffed down each leg, he could loop them over his bike like saddlebags for the ride home.

He was feeling hungry after all his efforts so he pulled out one of his sandwiches and sat down to eat. He chewed slowly, savoring each bite. Looking at the watch Manny had given him he found that he had spent hours dawdling along the trail and hadn't even realized he was hungry. It was now four o'clock but still too early for gigging.

A few yards in front of him, a pair of iridescent blue dragonflies flitted in tandem above the water and briefly hovered over the snout of an alligator sleeping in a patch of water lilies. Nearby, a frog had laid its eggs in neat rows along a tall spike of saw grass. The sun shining through the translucent white orbs illuminated the tiny tadpoles wriggling around inside. They would soon hatch and when they did, they would drop into the water below. Only a few would be lucky enough to escape being eaten by a turtle or gar and survive to become adults.

When he had finished his lunch, he settled down to read until dark. Books on flying had become his current favorites, and he pulled

An Aviator's Luck from his bedroll. When the light grew too dim to read, he set to work lighting the lantern.

Had it not been for the money, he wouldn't have had the stomach for gigging frogs. For one thing, once you had killed and skinned one, you kind of lost your taste for them. Besides that, it was pretty much like shooting fish in a barrel. The frogs really didn't have a fighting chance. You'd shine the lantern into the saw grass until you picked up the glow of frogs' eyes. Blinded by the light, the frogs just sat there paralyzed and waited for you to gig them. There wasn't much sport in that.

Eddie worked his way down the catwalk, and within an hour his sack was half-full—surely enough frogs to make his mother's dinner party a success. He pulled the pajama drawstring tight and tied it securely. He wedged the knotted ends of the string through a split in a warped board and hung the bag in the shallow water where the frogs would stay cool and wet until morning.

With a pleasantly full stomach and the sweet aftertaste of the chocolate bar still on his tongue, he stretched out on the dock to stargaze for a while before crawling into his tent to sleep. The night sounds sank from his consciousness, and suddenly it was dawn.

A rhythmic splashing of oars woke him up. He raised his head to scan the horizon for the source of the sound. At first he couldn't see a thing. Then he was able to follow a shimmer of ripples to their source—a rowboat cutting through the saw grass. It was still a good distance from him, and in the dim light Eddie could see three men in the skiff silhouetted against the lightening sky.

The boat slowed, and one of the occupants leaned out to tie the bowline to a cypress knee at the base of a big tree. The other slipped over the side into the water to steady them. Eddie was just about to get up and wave but suddenly stopped. The man still in the boat was roughly hauling the third man to his feet.

Suddenly, as if his eyes had become powerful field glasses, Eddie focused on the face of the prisoner. His hands tied, he sat slumped forward. Eddie could see the flat profile of his face etched against the pink glow of the sky. He recognized the badly broken nose and checkered suit—the very one he had been wearing that first day Eddie had seen him unloading the bootleg liquor.

The man turned and spoke to his captors. They paused to confer for a moment and then allowed him to settle himself back on the plank seat. Eddie listened hard trying to hear what they were saying. The morning air was thick and heavy. Sound was distorted as if they were speaking underwater. He could make out only the rise and fall of their voices, which seemed unnaturally slow, low-pitched and gravelly. The phonograph needs winding, he thought, hearing his mother's voice. In contrast, Manny's words came out strangely high and hoarse. The men stopped for a moment. Eddie ducked his head and lay as flat as possible but continued to watch, unable to stop himself from looking. Had Manny convinced them to abandon their mission and let him go?

The man beside Manny in the boat squatted down at his feet and methodically began to untie the big man's shoes. An icy shiver raised the hairs on the back of Eddie's neck, and he couldn't suppress a groan as he watched him calmly remove first one shoe and then the other, pause to wipe off a speck of dirt with a handkerchief, and then neatly place them next to Manny on the seat.

With this final act of mercy complete, the two forced him over the side and into waist-deep water, looped a rope around him, and then wound it around the trunk of the large tree. Eddie strained to see Manny's face, but his head was turned away.

Eddie didn't think he had ever seen the other two men before, but they were professionals. The brevity of their words and economy of their motions underscored their seriousness and knowledge. Once they had Manny securely bound, one reached into the back of the rowboat. He hoisted a bait bucket over the side. Wading over to where Manny stood, he calmly splashed the bucket of bloody water and fish guts over his shoulders and into the water around him.

Manny slumped over, his bowed head almost touching the water. He spoke again softly and began to sob, his big shoulders shuddering. Then he was quiet.

The two climbed back into the boat and rowed off just as calmly as they had come. In a few minutes, they and the skiff had disappeared from sight through the thick saw grass.

Countless gruesome scenarios swirled around in Eddie's head. The maelstrom sucked all the energy from his limbs leaving him as immobile as a stone. How could he help Manny? He would have to think quickly.

One idea after another presented itself, but he immediately cast each one aside as foolish, impractical or impossible. The distance between Manny's tree and the catwalk was at least two hundred yards across a swamp filled with water moccasins and alligators. He had no boat, no way to get to him.

The swamp was not the ocean. Eddie knew the ocean and was familiar with its dangers. In spite of its perils, the knowledge alone gave him some degree of confidence. He knew most sharks wouldn't attack without provocation, and if one came too close, a fist on the nose was usually enough to discourage him. Even more disturbing was the swamp water. It was dark and murky and filled with living flotsam, unlike the clear, clean water of the ocean. He had had little experience with alligators except for seeing one snap up a large dog that had waded into the shallows after a stick. Eddie remembered its howls for weeks afterward. He had also seen what the bite of a water moccasin could do to a grown man. Jim's father had been bitten when he was clearing a low-lying piece of land where a neighbor had been planning to build a dock. Within two hours, his arm had swollen to three times its original size and turned completely black. Before the poison ran its course, he had begun to hallucinate and very nearly died.

Eddie had to do something. But fear was riveting him to the spot. He lay immobile on the hard boards of the catwalk wanting to hide, to disappear. He couldn't just lie here and let Manny be torn apart by alligators. He had to *DO* something.

He heard his watch ticking away the seconds as he lay on the boards. He pressed his ear into the sound as it beat out each separate, purposeful second like a huge drumming metronome. For a moment, it eclipsed the pounding of his heart, and he felt a calm detachment as he fell to counting the clicks of its movement. The world slowed bringing each instant into a keen kind of focus. An insect landed on his arm. Sweat rivulets ran down his face, but he didn't feel the heat. The water below the catwalk rippled. The smell of rotting timbers beneath him filled his nostrils. Between the boards, he spied the glint of a Jesus bug riding the waves.

While Eddie lay immobile as a mosquito trapped in amber, Manny seemed to come to his senses. His panic-stricken face scanned the swirling chum spreading out through the water around his feet. His chest rose and fell with the force of bellows. Although it had been only a minute or two since the boat had disappeared, time in his world was moving all too fast.

Why, Eddie asked himself, did he have to be here on this day at this moment? This short introspective marked by guilt and terror came to a peak in the pivotal second when the sound began.

It started as a low, pitiful moan that slowly rose to a shriek. Several more screams followed. The last one abruptly ended in a gurgling gasp as his head went under. A tremendous splashing followed.

Gators prefer to eat underwater. They grip their prey in their strong jaws and legs, and roll their powerful bodies over and over, dragging it beneath the surface. In seconds, the roiling water was stained dark red, and Eddie raised his head just in time to see a leg swathed in brown and white checked cloth float to the surface.

Another scream edged into his consciousness, an agonized, wrenching cry. Where was the sound coming from? "Stop it! Stop it!" He covered his ears and then realized the sound was coming from his own mouth. And, as if a veil had been drawn, blackness fell.

Slowly his mind began to process small details—the coolness of the boards of the catwalk under his belly, the screech of a hawk circling high overhead. He turned to look out across the shallows and winced when a sharp crick in his neck brought him to a painful and sudden awareness. The pressure of his cheek against the watch had left a deep impression on his face and the flesh of his wrist. The position of the watch hands and the sun confirmed that he had been out here all night.

Trying to reassure himself, he looked out across the swamp. Maybe the scene he had witnessed was a dream or his imagination. Maybe it was a product of his growing sense of isolation or the remoteness of this place. His stomach lurched when the image of Manny's torn body bobbing on the surface of the bloodstained water reappeared in his mind. "God!" he cried out sobbing.

*   *   *

"I looked down and there was the bag of frogs where I'd left it. I grabbed it up and I . . . just ran, I ran, I ran . . . away," he sobbed.

Ed drew in a ragged breath and several gasps between agonized, incoherent phrases. A film of perspiration glistened on his face. Tears stained his cheeks and fell to his chest.

"Manny, what could I do? What could I do?" he murmured to himself, still locked inside the memory. Diana held his hand and listened until he calmed, collapsed back onto his pillow, and finally fell into an exhausted sleep.

What could she say about such horror? Nothing. Simply nothing.

On Wednesday morning, two weeks after his stroke, Diana signed his release papers. Pausing for a moment to thank the staff and tuck the folder of warnings and instructions into the carryall with his clothes, she took his hand as a nurse wheeled him toward the elevator.

Outside, the breeze off the water smelled pure and fresh, cleansed of the stale antiseptic odors of the hospital. Ed drew in a deep breath and smiled. His story wasn't quite finished yet, though. He vowed to himself that today he would finish it completely. Crossing the bridge on the ride home, he silently mulled over the last untold details. In a way, this last would be the hardest part to explain. Bridges. Would the carefully constructed one he was about to cross be strong enough to bear the weight of the final revelation?

TWENTY-NINE

Though the afternoon was warm, a light breeze sent a flurry of dry leaves scuttling along the walk and ruffled the American flag in the front yard as Diana and Ed pulled into the drive.

"I don't think this old place has ever looked as good to me as it does today," Ed said with a grin. "Even the peeling paint on the shutters."

"I have a surprise for you, Dad," Diana said, ushering him through the living room and toward the back porch. She pushed the screen door open and held it as he stepped outside. "What do you think?" She gestured toward two newly planted umbrella trees that now provided a spot of shade on the corner where the swing hung. He looked at the sturdy young trees and smiled.

"Well, they look just fine, don't they?" he said, reaching out to rub one of the big shiny leaves between his thumb and forefinger. As they sat in the shade eating Cuban sandwiches Diana had made that morning, Ed began again hesitantly.

"I remember running, but I still don't remember how they found me," Ed explained. "All I remember was the darkness. Sometimes there were voices, strange noises, footsteps. They scared me. I thought if I didn't move or make a sound I'd be safe. But every so often, the voices came back again. Different voices. I wanted them to leave me alone. I squeezed my eyes shut. I knew I shouldn't open them. Not then, not ever."

*　　　　*　　　　*

A hand grazed his brow. He felt something wet run across his face. A brief fluttering ensued, then it was quiet again. His mind continued to float in the dark space. He couldn't calculate how much time had passed before he began to come around and wonder where he was.

He began to focus on the noises he heard and tried to identify them. He couldn't remember anything but darkness. He felt cramped and stiff. With grim determination and great effort, he tried to open his eyes. Narrow slits of light forced their way through dark bars, which he watched curiously. Little by little, the bars grew farther apart as his eyelashes slowly parted. Dimness replaced total darkness.

He wiggled his toes against the tight tent covering them. As if he were slowly being immersed in a warm bath, he became aware of his body again. He began to feel his feet, hands, then his limbs, until he was fully aware of his whole body. He was enclosed within a tight cocoon. He still couldn't see anything, but he now realized that his head was also encased within the same thin fabric covering. A vague feeling of terror gripped him. Tentatively, he tugged the cloth away from his face.

He looked around. He was lying on a small bed in an unfamiliar space surrounded by a pale green curtain. His neck hurt when he turned his head, and his stomach muscles ached as they did after a hundred sit-ups. A hand reached out and touched his chest, and he flinched.

"Eddie." It was his father's voice, but it sounded cracked and unnatural.

"Eddie, it's okay now. You're safe."

With painful determination, he turned his head toward the voice. His father was sitting on a small chair next to the bed leaning toward him. His face looked haggard and anxious. His eyes were red as if he hadn't slept in a long time.

"You've come back to us," he said.

"Where . . . how did I get here?"

"A couple of fishermen found you passed out on a trail leading out of the Glades. You'd been missing for two days. Your mother and I have been sick with worry. We've been taking turns sitting by you waiting for you to wake up. For the last four days, though, you've been curled up under the sheets. You wouldn't even bring your head out from under. But you're okay now, son." He smiled in a way Eddie had never seen him smile before.

*   *   *

"You know how you hear people experience amnesia after something awful happens, Diana?" Ed asked, pausing to swallow the last of his iced tea. "It's true. I experienced it. For days after I ran down that catwalk, I didn't know anything. My mind just shut down. But when I came out of it and the doctors released me, my father took me home. That was when the longest and most agonizing month of my life began."

"Don't you think you should rest now?" Diana stopped him, looking for signs of stress.

"No, I'm okay," he said. He closed his eyes and let his mind slide back into the past, searching for the words that would help her understand.

*   *   *

Fearful of what might come, Eddie wouldn't sleep, yet he refused to leave his bed. Food turned his stomach. It seemed that nothing could erase the scene that played and replayed itself in his mind until every detail was etched there with sharp clarity. Still anxious, his parents asked the doctor to make a house call. After a second thorough examination, the doctor concluded that he could find nothing physically wrong with him. He assured Eddie's worried parents that a couple of nights alone in the Glades would be enough to have a severe effect on anyone. Just give him time, he said.

During the next weeks, Eddie could think of nothing but Manny. He kept going over and over his one regret; Manny had trusted him to deliver the letter to Diaz, and Eddie had let him down. Whatever had happened to Manny was on Eddie's conscience. It was his fault. He was sure of it. Whenever he allowed his thoughts to wander, the comment Manny had made to him after the horse races kept running through his mind with a cruel tinge of irony. "Come on, Eddie," Manny had said. "Don't take it personal. It's just the way life is."

He continued to suffer in silence. Only after long weeks that followed did he slowly begin to return to some semblance of normalcy. Even though at first he had to force himself to leave his bed and will his body to carry on with the functions of simple existence, by slow degrees life resumed.

Jim came to see him every day. He talked, they played cribbage, and finally Eddie began to recover bits and pieces of his old self. They started to think about looking for summer jobs. Eddie knew the pay wouldn't be great, but at least he'd be able to sleep at night.

One afternoon several weeks later, Eddie and Jim rode their bikes out to the Pan Am barge to put in applications for work as baggage loaders. While they waited in the passenger lounge for the dock boss,

Eddie idly glanced through a newspaper lying on the counter. An article on the bottom of the front page caught his eye.

The Miami Herald

Dade County Police Continue Search for Missing Witness

Police continue their search for Manny Silver, who had been scheduled to testify before the Dade County Grand Jury in May. Silver had been subpoenaed to testify for the prosecution in the state's case against accused mob boss Al Capone. When Silver failed to appear in court, police searched his residence, where they found evidence of a struggle. A search to locate Mr. Silver has turned up nothing thus far, and after several weeks there have been no leads.

Jim craned his neck, reading over Eddie's shoulder.

"Well, what goes around comes around," Jim said with a shrug.

Eddie read the article again before slowly folding the paper and setting it on the counter. For a long time he said nothing, struggling to unclench the cold hand that had wrapped itself around his chest. The room began to shimmer before his eyes. He tried to stifle a shuddering breath and abruptly turned his back to Jim pretending to watch a Sikorsky motoring in across the bay.

*   *   *

The liquid trill of a mockingbird broke the late afternoon silence. From the porch swing Diana and Ed watched the orange sun slowly emerge from behind a patch of shifting purple clouds as it dropped toward the horizon. Ed sighed.

"I guess that newspaper article confirmed what I'd hoped was my imagination. It was right after that day that the terrible nightmares began. The police never found Manny's body, so the case eventually became just another unsolved disappearance. But I've seen that scene played out over and over again ever since. All these years, the dreams never really stopped. But since you came, I've started getting a few more nights sleep," he said it with a self-deprecating laugh.

Diana slid her arm through his. "So, it wasn't fishing you were dreaming about, but Manny from all those years ago," she stated matter-of-factly.

"I thought I'd carry the story to my grave," he said, his gaze lost someplace deep within himself. "But, yes, and now I've burdened you with it. You wanted to know me. So now it's your story. It's too late for me to make amends to your mother, but at least now you know why she left me. How could I expect her to understand? She gave me everything she could, but I didn't think she could continue to love me if she knew the truth. How would she forgive me if I couldn't forgive myself?"

Diana took his hand in hers as they sat silently in the soft peach glow of the setting sun, both lost in their own thoughts.

Straightening his shoulders, Ed turned and with a sense of resolution looked deeply into Diana's eyes for a moment before he spoke.

"These nightmares have been my own private purgatory where I've done penance all the years since Manny's disappearance. Do you want to leave now that you know? If you do, I'll understand."

Diana smiled. "What do you think?" She looked at him with an earnestly questioning face. Her expression brought a bubble of memory to the surface—his many talks with Father Horka.

Ed could still hear Father Horka's voice and the words he'd spoken with such unshakable faith and conviction those many years ago: "*Whether one's sins are willful and intentional or simply the result of ignorance or weakness, it is our acknowledgement of guilt and our acceptance of responsibility for a wrong done that eventually cleanses the soul and helps us find peace.*"

The story was finished now. The fresh breeze that rustled the trees carried with it the smell of the sea. He breathed in deeply. Two tall palms stood silhouetted against a bank of lavender clouds. This evening's sunset promised to be an especially beautiful one.

EPILOGUE

That summer Eddie and Jim got jobs as baggage handlers for Pan American's new airline. The following year after graduation, Eddie worked his way into a full-time position in the burgeoning airline, and Jim went off to college.

Eddie heard from Estelle just once. She wrote to tell him she was married to a great guy who worked for her father. He reminded her of Eddie, she said.

The federal government didn't indict Al Capone until 1931 when they finally arrested him for income tax evasion. He was sent to a prison in Pennsylvania where he worked the system and continued to live like a king.

On March 1, 1932, the baby son of Colonel and Mrs. Charles Lindbergh was kidnapped. They grieved, and the nation grieved with them. A new law was passed making kidnapping a federal crime.

1933 saw the repeal of The Eighteenth Amendment ending mob control of the lucrative whiskey business. In February of that same year, Franklin Delano Roosevelt came to Miami with Chicago's Mayor Anton Cermak to make a speech. A small, olive skinned man brandishing a pistol darted toward the dais where Roosevelt was speaking, and before anyone could stop him, he climbed on a chair and fired off several shots. The shots missed Roosevelt but hit Cermak squarely in the chest. Guiseppe Zangara, an out of work Italian anarchist, had lost money at the dog track and tried to kill Roosevelt because he wanted to get even with capitalists. He might have succeeded, too, had he not lost his balance. Cermak died two weeks later, and Zangara was sentenced to die in the electric chair. If Guissepe Zangara's aim had been more accurate, Roosevelt would not have lived to lead the nation to victory over Hitler in the coming war.

In 1935, the government created The Works Progress Administration to provide jobs for the unemployed through improving national parks, planting trees, and building walks, roads and bridges. Some of that money was appropriated for a project in Key West, and several hundred veterans were loaded on trains to be taken there to work.

No one knew the next hurricane would strike south of Miami. Storm warnings for the Keys were delayed in a snarl of government red tape. By the time a train was dispatched to bring the vets back to the mainland, winds had reached hurricane force in the Keys. The loaded trains already heading north were swept into the ocean like confetti. The force of the wind and water left long sections of steel rail wound up like corkscrews. When the storm was over, nothing remained of the overseas railroad except the concrete foundations imbedded in the coral rock seabed. The center of the storm passed over Matacumbe Key sweeping away everything but a few concrete floors also attached to the bedrock. Almost no one was spared. Bodies were found jammed into the mangrove roots and branches of the few remaining trees. Some could be removed only by sawing them into pieces. The only way to reach the destruction was by boat. As bodies were recovered, they were placed in hastily constructed wooden boxes and brought by boat to the railroad on the mainland for shipping. The boxes were not airtight, and the smell of death drifted for miles on the breeze.

Another building boom followed the real estate crash. It resulted in a rapidly growing sewage problem. The solution was to invade the ocean fifty feet out into the bay where the waters became a giant septic tank. Not long after, many of the sponges and coral began to die of disease and pollution. The fish population declined and the once pure bay lost its crystal clarity, becoming murky gray.

In 1934 Capone was transferred to Alcatraz. For years he had lived with an untreated STD. After being diagnosed with advanced syphilis dementia, he was released in 1939 to spend his remaining years at his home in Miami Beach where he sat in his robe fishing off his docked boat. He was often confused and sometimes wandered off the grounds and walked aimlessly around the neighborhood.

After the attack on Pearl Harbor, Jim enlisted in the Navy and was sent to fight in the Pacific theater. When a Japanese torpedo struck his ship, he was killed along with most of the other seamen onboard. If a person could choose his manner of death, Jim would have chosen to die in the ocean he loved so much.

In the fifties, a concerted effort was made to clean up the bay. Things began to look much better until Kennedy's Bay of Pigs. After Castro had secured his hold on Cuba, Kennedy assuaged his guilt for the debacle by granting asylum to all Cubans who could make it to the Florida shores. They came by the uncounted thousands. To the Cuban fisherman, Biscayne Bay was heaven. Without the constraints of conservation laws, some operated fleets of fishing boats dragging bottom nets, and in short order stripped the bay of nearly all remaining fish and shrimp.

During the last quarter century, Miami has become a melting pot much like El Paso and Los Angeles but with a strongly Caribbean flavor. Fruit carts selling mangos and guavas have replaced the frozen custard stands of the old days. Eighth Street, now known as Calle Ocho, is crowded with tiny cafes where old men relax in the evenings playing dominoes and sipping tiny cups of strong expresso. Today, Greater Miami is a city of over two and half million people who are a culturally diverse population. Over 50% of its present citizens were born outside of the U.S., coming principally from Cuba and the Caribbean. Nearly 70% speak a language other than English in their homes.

Downtown Miami, East Flagler Street, 1926
Credit: State Archives of Florida

Central arcade—Miami, Florida, 1922
Credit: State Archives of Florida

Federal agents pouring bootleg liquor down the sewer.
Credit: Library of Congress, Seagram Collection

Coast Guard cutter blown ashore, 1926
Credit: State Archives of Florida

Sonny Capone's birthday party
Credit: Arva Parks Moore & Co.

Al Capone's older brother
Credit: Mario Gomes MyCaponeMuseum.com

Pan American S-40 seaplane at Dinner Key
Credit: State Archives of Florida

View of Everglades from the Tamiami Trail
Credit: State Archives of Florida

Al Capone's elegant jail cell in Eastern State Penitentiary,
Philadelphia, PA
Credit: Wikipedia.com

Funeral for victims of 1935 Hurricane
Credit: State Archives of Florida